WILDE, NE\

A Wilde Wedding Night
Her Two Wilde Billionaire Bad Boys

Chloe Lang

MENAGE EVERLASTING

Siren Publishing, Inc.
www.SirenPublishing.com

A SIREN PUBLISHING BOOK
IMPRINT: Ménage Everlasting

WILDE, NEVADA
A Wilde Wedding Night
Her Two Wilde Billionaire Bad Boys
Copyright © 2014 by Chloe Lang

ISBN: 978-1-62741-227-8

First Printing: May 2014

A Wilde Wedding Night
Her Two Wilde Billionaire Bad Boys
    Cover design by Les Byerley
Print cover design by Siren-BookStrand
All art and logo copyright © 2014 by Siren Publishing, Inc.

Printed in the U.S.A.

PUBLISHER
Siren Publishing, Inc.
www.SirenPublishing.com

DEDICATIONS

A Wilde Wedding Night

There's three people that helped me greatly with this visit to the past in Wilde, Nevada.

Lanae LeMore was by my side the entire time. I can't wait to see you published. No more excuses. You have real talent.

Sophie Oak kept me from rambling on and on with this one. You are a wonderful friend and mentor.

Chloe Vale keeps me moving forward. You're a doll.

Her Two Wilde Billionaire Bad Boys

This one is dedicated to a woman who has been in my life longer than anyone. She's my mentor, my hero, my example of how one should live their life to the fullest, and my friend.

Mom, this one is for you.

SIREN
Publishing

Ménage Everlasting

A Wilde Wedding Night

REVISED &
EXPANDED

Chloe Lang

A WILDE WEDDING NIGHT

CHLOE LANG
Copyright © 2014

San Francisco – July 1951

Sitting in a booth by the window in the diner, Carol Faxon put down the letter she'd read a dozen times already.

She needed a cup of coffee after finishing her last final. She had stayed up until 1:30 a.m. making sure she was ready for the exam. She needed to be at school at 7:00, so there had been no time for breakfast, much less coffee. Knowing she had aced the final, she could now relax.

It had been a long time since she'd gotten a letter from Mrs. Baker, and this one was a big surprise. The sweet woman's words made her cry. Mrs. Baker congratulated her over finishing college and advised her to take time to have some fun before jumping into the next chapter of life.

Graduation was only a couple of days away. She wasn't going to attend the ceremony. Not without her longtime, loving mentor in the audience. Besides, it was time to have fun. Mrs. Baker's letter said so.

"What can I get you, miss?" a waitress asked her.

"Coffee for now."

"You got it." The woman walked away, leaving Carol to her thoughts.

Fun? What kind of fun, Mrs. Baker? "Now what do I do with my life?"

Although there were many opportunities, none of them seemed right for her. Nothing seemed to fit. Considering her upbringing, maybe that was to be expected. Mrs. Baker's most repeated message during their chats went through her mind.

Never look down on anyone, Carol. Never let anyone look down on you, either. Look everyone straight in the eyes. You're as worthy of respect and happiness as anyone else.

Mrs. Baker had included that mantra in her letter, along with many more of her life lessons. The final message scrawled in the dear lady's handwriting was a quote from Napoleon Hill.

To be a star, you must shine your own light, follow your own path, and don't worry about the darkness, for that is when the stars shine brightest

God, she missed her.

As Carol looked around the room she spotted a good-looking soldier, who reminded her a lot of Gary Cooper.

Wow. I would love to meet someone like him and live happily ever after.

She made herself laugh at the thought. The soldier turned around to leave, noticed her looking at him, and their eyes locked.

Oh my God, he's coming over here.

"Hi, ma'am. My name is Jack Wilde. I was wondering if I could join you."

Since this was a very public place, she decided why not. After all, wasn't she just wishing to meet him? It nearly made her giggle.

I must be very tired.

"Company would be nice, soldier."

Jack sat down across from her. His smile was broad and inviting. "Thank you, miss."

"It's Carol, Mr. Wilde."

The handsome man extended his hand.

She shook it, realizing how tiny her fingers looked next to his.

"Nice to meet you, Carol." Jack winked. "I prefer 'Jack' from my friends."

"Friends? We just met. Do your lines like that work on all the girls?"

"Never tried this one on anyone else. How am I doing so far?"

She laughed, feeling more comfortable with him. "Ask me after I get my coffee, Jack."

"You've got a deal."

Two cups later, Carol was ready to tell him his lines worked just fine.

Jack began telling her why he was in San Francisco. He'd just gotten back from his tour of duty overseas. His brothers had come in late last night from Wilde, Nevada, to take him home. Tom and Will had been so beaten from the drive that Jack had suggested they sleep in while he went to get his morning coffee.

She and Jack continued talking, and before they realized, it was lunchtime. He told her he was so excited to meet her and that he would like to get to know her better.

Jack said, "Why don't we eat lunch and I'll tell you more about me and my brothers."

"You think they're actually still asleep?" she asked.

He nodded. "I can't wait for you to meet them. Carol, you're going to knock their socks off."

She felt heat in her cheeks. "How about we keep this to one-on-one for now?"

Jack sipped his coffee, but didn't answer. "They're great guys. You're going to like them. You'll see."

He continued telling her about Tom and Will. They were hardworking cowboys, just like Jack had been before joining the Army. He was extremely anxious to get back to the life he loved. Jack's brotherly bond could be heard in every syllable he uttered.

"You've just got to meet them, Carol. What do you say?"

After contemplating on this for a second, she nodded. "Okay." Still unsure she should give Jack her address until she knew him better, she said, "I'll join you at The Lone Star club at eight thirty tonight. It's a country-western type club. I think you and your brothers, being cowboys, would enjoy the atmosphere."

After finishing their lunch, they said their good-byes.

"I'll see you at eight thirty, Carol."

She went back to her apartment feeling lighter and more carefree than she had in ages.

The time between lunch and her walk to The Lone Star had been filled with her continually bringing up images of Jack Wilde sitting across from her in their booth at the diner.

At 8:30, she entered the club.

There he was, Jack, standing with two more of the most handsome men she'd ever seen in her life.

God, is this real? I wish there were three of me. How could anyone choose a man from that trio?

"Carol, I'd like to introduce you to my brothers. This is Will."

Will could've passed for Cary Grant's twin. "Nice to meet you, Carol."

Jack put his arm around her shoulder, giving her a tiny tingle.

"So this must be Tom," she said to the other brother, who reminded her of Tyrone Power.

"How about we sit and get to know one another?" Tom asked.

"I'd like that very much."

As they began to talk, it seemed as though she'd known them for years. Usually a nervous wreck around men, these three put her at ease immediately.

Jack asked her to dance, and as they were very close, he touched her lips softly, which sent off sparks from the top of her head to the tips of her toes. She let him kiss her deeper, responding with pure pleasure.

She imagined being with Jack the rest of her life. *I simply must be losing my mind. We only just met this morning.* Regardless, it was a nice thought.

When the club started to close, Carol decided it would be okay for them to walk her home. They had been perfect gentlemen, and besides, Jack was a soldier, which eased her worry.

When they got to her door, Jack kissed her again, this time more passionately, which drove her into ecstasy.

No one had made her feel like this before. No one ever.

Before she had a chance to collect her thoughts, Tom leaned over and kissed her, too, followed by Will. They both gave her the same tingles as she'd received from Jack. *This is absolutely impossible. How can I have such excitement over three men?*

It must've been the beer for all four of them.

Carol walked into her house, closing the door, pausing for a moment to reflect on what just happened. No answers, none, nothing.

Quit trying to understand, Carol. Just enjoy yourself. That's what Mrs. Baker would say. Of course the woman would say it in her own special way.

Graduation came and went. She hadn't even thought about the ceremony, relishing the time she spent with the three cowboys from Wilde, a town whose name they shared. With them always as her companions, every hour flew by. They went to movies, the beach, museums, and at night they would go to The Lone Star and dance.

Carol didn't understand her feelings for all three cowboys. She actually thought she was falling in love with the most wonderful men…*Did I say men?*

It was true, but simply not possible.

* * * *

Looking up at the stars in the San Francisco sky, Jack squeezed Carol's hand. She squeezed back, which made him happy. It was a perfect night for a picnic.

Tom looked at his watch. "We better get going if we're going to make it before the band starts playing."

"Why do you guys have to take me to The Lone Star when the doors open? I'm only one woman."

Will grabbed her free hand. "Exactly. We're three cowboys who have to share you. We each only get a third of the dances you get."

She laughed. "That's why I have to soak my legs in a hot bath every night after you take me home."

"Do you need a night away from the club, baby?" Jack asked. "We could grab some beer and come back here. That sound fun to you?"

Tom nodded. "The weather is nice tonight."

She shook her head. "No. I love to dance and I don't want you to stop taking me. This is the most fun I've had since my first year in college."

"You heard the lady," Tom said. "Let's get to The Lone Star."

"I'd like that," she said. "But can we just stay a little longer and talk?"

"Done, sweetheart." Jack and his brothers had spent every waking moment with her, and he wasn't about to disappoint her of anything she wanted.

She sighed. "Tell me more about your home back in Wilde."

He kissed her on the cheek. "We've told you so many stories about our childhood I think you know them better than we do now."

"It sounds like such a wonderful place to grow up. I could listen to you talk about it all night."

Will laughed. "But you have, Carol. Many nights."

"He's right, doll." Jack sensed Carol had trouble with her past, as she'd told them only about coming to San Francisco to go to college. When pressed to talk about anything before, she'd changed the subject. He hated to push her, but knew that if they had any chance of winning her heart, she needed to trust them with her darkest secrets, no matter how painful they were. "You promised to tell us something about your childhood. Fair is fair.

"I suppose I should tell you. It's just hard." She closed her eyes. "I didn't have the happy times you guys had."

"Maybe we should save this for another day," Tom said, concern written all over his face.

He loved his brother for being so tender with Carol, but now wasn't the time. "Nope. We've waited to hear her story." He cupped her chin. "No matter how hard or terrible it is, Carol. We're here for you. I promise." He kissed her tenderly on the lips.

"I believe you, Jack." She took in a deep breath, and then began. "I've never told anyone this before. No one. It is fair for you to know. God, how I wish I'd had the kind of home you guys did, but I didn't. My parents were drunks, plain and simple. During my childhood, they would do anything for a drink, including selling their own wretched bodies."

Even though he'd suspected trouble from her past, he had no idea how bad it had been for Carol.

"So many nights I was left alone in my parents' old scary farmhouse with all its creaks and noises."

"How old were you then?" he asked, rage building for the horrible upbringing Carol had to endure.

"Not even school age. My mind would race whenever I was by myself, imagining all kinds of scary monsters inside the house. I would lock myself in the bathroom where I remained until my mom and dad came back from wherever they'd gone. Even though I was petrified at being alone, I never knew what to expect when they returned. Sometimes they would just pass out on the bed, but more often than not they would come in fighting.

"Did they ever hit you, sweetheart?" Will said between clenched teeth.

She shrugged. "Sometimes they came in all happy and laughing. Other times they would hit me, angry because I hadn't cleaned up their mess."

Jack's gut tightened, imagining Carol's fucking parents beating her.

"When I turned eight, the monsters in my mind became imaginary bad men, who would come in with knives or guns trying to find me so they could kill me. But on my tenth birthday, the real nightmare came. My parents decided it was time for me to earn my keep. Being raised by them, I had a pretty good idea what that meant. I ran away several times, but the neighbors would find me and bring me back."

As tears fell from her eyes, Jack vowed silently to himself to do whatever he had to do to keep Carol's monsters away. He pulled her into him tight. "We're here with you, baby."

"I'm glad you're here, guys. This is hard to talk about, but it's good to let it out."

"Take your time, sweetheart," Tom said.

She nodded. "In a drunken stupor, my parents brought me to their favorite bar to sell...my...my virginity to the highest bidder."

Fuck!

"Fortunately, there was an off-duty cop at the bar having a beer. He saw my parents trying to auction me off. The officer immediately called for backup, and my parents were hauled away in handcuffs. That was the last time I ever saw them." Carol wiped her eyes. "I was taken to the orphanage. What do you think of your Little Orphan Annie, fellows?"

Your? "I think she's incredible," Jack said. "Go on, baby. What happened there?"

"I was so scared, not knowing what to expect. But even though it wasn't the easiest of places to spend one's childhood, it was several steps up from how I'd been living with my parents. I never was alone again sitting on the floor behind a locked door waiting and worrying what hell would show up. Getting me to school had never been a priority for my mom and dad, so even though the teachers at the orphanage were extremely strict, they were very kind and encouraged me on every aspect of my life. My studies improved until I was at the top of my class. According to Mrs. Baker, the headmistress, I was the best girl she'd ever had there. I never back talked anyone. I always kept my space neat and clean. I did my chores with a smile. I'd never been happier."

"You deserved happiness after all you went through," Jack said.

"Mrs. Baker was like a grandmother to me. She and I had many long talks. She told me that because I was going to be on my own at eighteen, I needed a good education to support myself. She's the one who encouraged me to attend college. I began to dream of that day. At sixteen, I started working at a local diner. I saved every penny and had enough to start college in the fall of my eighteenth year. I had to work all through school, but I made enough to pay for education, rent, and all other expenses."

"Mrs. Baker sounds like a wonderful woman," Jack said.

"She *was*. She always talked about attending my graduation, but she died last year. I didn't go to the ceremony. That's just a formality anyway. Besides, I would've had to skip a night with you guys."

"I would've gone to see you get your diploma, Carol," Will said.

Tom added, "We all would have."

"I know, but I wanted to dance with you, not walk across a stuffy stage."

"I wish your Mrs. Baker had been here to see what an amazing woman you've become." Jack brushed the hair out of her eyes.

"In a way, she was. I received a letter from her a couple of days before the graduation ceremony. I was reading it when you came over that first morning at the diner, Jack." Carol smiled, a single tear trailing down her cheek. "Before she died, she'd set it up with someone at the orphanage to send me the letter after I graduated as her way of being there that day. It's my most precious possession."

"Sounds priceless to me," Tom said. "Like you, Carol."

"Sweet talker." She jumped up. "I think that's enough talking for tonight. My feet are itching to dance."

"Your wish is our command, love," Will said.

They packed up their picnic items, blanket and all, and headed to The Lone Star club.

Jack put his arm around the woman he'd fallen head over heels for. He, Tom, and Will had already decided to stay in San Francisco as long as they must to win Carol's heart. After tonight, he would stay until the end of time if need be. She belonged with them. She belonged in Wilde.

* * * *

Carol took another drink of the cool water. Thankfully, the shot of penicillin the doctor had given her for her sinus infection seemed to be working. She could breathe more clearly, but her ears were still stopped up.

"Another dance, baby?" Jack sure knew how to have fun.

She shook her head. "I'm not sure my feet can take another dance, fellows."

His brothers, Tom and Will, looked disappointed.

Tom said, "Doll, it's only midnight. Rest up a couple of songs, and then I'll spin you around the dance floor. What do you say?"

As if on cue, the band fired up another tune that made hearing the brothers even harder. Will put his arm around her shoulders.

Tom said something again, but she wasn't quite sure what with her ears in their current condition and the music and crowd being so rowdy and loud. Trying to concentrate was becoming a challenge tonight. She'd awoken this morning with her sinuses giving her fits. Knowing this was her last night with the three sexy brothers, she took the only open appointment her doctor had left in the middle of the afternoon. She hadn't told the guys about it. Three weeks ago, she'd been a little under the weather, and they had made her go to bed and fed her chicken soup until she thought she would never be able to eat it again. She wasn't about to ruin this evening with a silly infection.

"Well, let me go first then, Carol." Jack got down on one knee. He took her hand in his. "My brothers and I may have only known you a short time, but you have captured our hearts."

"You have mine, too." She took a deep breath, hoping the medicine inside her would unstop her ears and fast. Jack said more, but she had missed it. She thought about asking him to repeat himself, but decided not to. One, it might tip him off that she wasn't feeling well. Two, she didn't want to spoil the moment. Finally, she wanted to appear strong and capable in front of these amazing men.

He paused, waiting for her to answer. What had he asked her? To marry him, no doubt. But could she be sure? She was shivering like a schoolgirl. This was no way a woman with a degree in biology from Stanford should be acting. *This is nineteen fifty-one and I'm a modern woman.*

She'd worked hard to finish college. Saying yes to a proposal would mean leaving all that behind. In truth, having a career had always been secondary in her heart, though she'd never admitted that to anyone. What she really had dreamed of for her whole life was having a husband and children. Her own family had always been distant and cold, so opposite these warm and loving cowboys.

"So, what do you say, baby? Will you marry *us*?"

She grinned at the irony that her stopped-up ears had twisted his words into an impossible dream, her impossible dream. She wouldn't have to choose. She'd fallen for all three brothers, but knew she could only have one. Tom's adventurous spirit, Will's sense of humor, and Jack's protective nature made the perfect combination to ensnare her utterly. How had this happened? Didn't women's hearts only go for one man? *What's wrong with me that I let this happen?*

Jack was on his knees in front of her, asking her to marry *him*, not *us*.

Stanford was behind her, and she was ready to choose a new path.

"I will," she answered, feeling nervous and excited about what was to come.

Each of the brothers kissed her. Of course, Tom's and Will's kisses must've been congratulatory in nature, nothing more. But they'd seemed a bit too intimate to her. She chalked it up to fatigue.

The rest of the evening was a haze. Each of the brothers took her out on the dance floor, one after another, over and over, until the crowd thinned and the band put up their instruments.

The last thing she remembered was the three hunky cowboys at her door, promising to be back early to pick her up and take her to their new home, *her* new home, in Wilde, Nevada. Just before her exhaustion pushed her into unconsciousness, she thought about what tomorrow would bring. She would be Mrs. Jack Wilde, which thrilled her. *But God help me, I love all three of them.*

* * * *

Wilde, Nevada – August 1951

Carol shivered, not from cold but from the gravity of the life-changing moment that was happening to her.

"Do you, Carol, take these men to be your husbands of heart, to love…"

Had she heard the justice of the peace correctly? *These men?* The trip from San Francisco had been long, but she'd slept almost the entire way. Thankfully, her sinuses and ears had cleared before the three Wilde brothers had shown up at her place to get her. So why was her hearing off? Must've been impacted by her nerves.

"…in sickness and in health, so long as you all shall live?"

"I do," she whispered.

"And do you, Jack, take this woman…"

Her fiancé of less than twenty-four hours, who was seconds away from being her husband, listened intently to the minister's long-winded question. He wore his Army dress uniform, khaki jacket, trousers, shirt, and black tie. He was stunning.

Wearing dark blue suits, crisp white shirts, and red ties, Tom and Will stood beside her and Jack.

She'd met the three brothers only a month ago. It had been a whirlwind romance, nights of dancing, delicious dinners, flowers, drinks, making out—God, could the men make a girl's toes curl—and so much more.

They'd become quite the foursome around town. Not surprising, since the Wilde brothers had leading-man good looks, though they were more cowboy than anything else. The silver screen would've loved them, but they were clearly meant for the saddle, which drew quite a lot of stares and invites from the San Francisco elite. Novelty could definitely open doors in the city, though those doors would close quickly once the movers and shakers moved on to the next oddity that captured their attention.

Glad to be done with college, Carol was ready for a new start, a new life. When Jack had asked her to marry him, she'd jumped at the chance. Sure, it had only been a month, but she was already in love with him. The way he, Tom, and Will talked about Wilde with such awe and devotion made her decision that much easier. God, those brothers had brought hope and light into her uncertain and gray life.

"I do," Jack vowed in his deep, rumbling tone. He had piercing blue eyes that had mesmerized her the first time she'd seen them. They still gave her a sweet shiver whenever he gazed at her.

"And do you, Tom, take this…"

God, what's wrong with me? There's no way I'm hearing the minister correctly. But Carol listened more closely to the man, realizing that she was hearing him just fine. What the hell was going on? A couple of weeks ago, she would've bet that Tom would've been the one to ask her to marry him, but he hadn't.

"I do," Tom answered.

Her heart jumped into overdrive in her chest.

"And do you, Will…"

Was this some kind of rural part of the ceremony where siblings had to make a vow to their brother's new bride? Who else would be vowing to love her? Their parents? Aunts and uncles? Her home state of Maine had its own set of odd customs, and she knew small-town quirkiness quite well growing up in Banksfield, population five hundred and ten. She would adjust just fine to Wilde and whatever traditions and superstitions it had. *In for a penny, in for a pound.*

"I do," Will said.

"Vows of love and commitment have been given here and witnessed by all gathered in this place. By the powers vested in me in the city of Wilde, Nevada, I now pronounce you married. Gentlemen, you may now kiss your bride."

Her mind spun like a child's top as Jack pulled her in close and kissed her. Every inch of her melted into her new husband, forgetting the odd way the minister had conducted the service. Things would be fine. She'd signed the marriage license, which only had one other name on it—Jack's. He was her husband, not Tom, not Will. Part of her was relieved as logic finally made clear what had actually occurred. But another part, a secret part, was disappointed. The truth was she would've said yes to a proposal from either Tom or Will, too.

"I love you, Carol." Jack's fixed stare made her weak in the knees.

Then he stepped aside, and Tom moved directly in front of her. "I love you too, sweetheart." He put his hands at the back of her neck and at the small of her waist and drew her body in close, placing his thick, manly lips on hers. *Oh God!* She closed her eyes as his kiss made her wonderfully woozy.

Am I still asleep in the back of Will's Cadillac Fleetwood, headed to Wilde, having a wicked dream? The choice had been made. She was marrying Jack, and yet she was kissing Tom like there was no tomorrow. *Shit!*

She opened her eyes and saw from their corners all the people in the chapel looking at them. They didn't seem shocked or appalled. In fact, many women were dotting their own eyes with hankies and those that weren't were smiling broadly. The men, too, seemed okay with this whole strange wedding.

When Tom ended their kiss, Will grabbed her and planted one helluva kiss on her. The spinning top in her mind went faster and faster until it broke out into a major storm, a hurricane with winds so strong everything in its path was flattened or blown away. She learned that things out west were much different than they'd been for her growing up in Maine, but Wilde made everything she'd seen in San Francisco seem tame.

She'd heard the minister correctly, and insane or not, she had jumped down the rabbit hole and just married three men.

* * * *

Jack kept his arm around his new bride. Carol was wide-eyed and so very quiet. Though he'd known her only a month, this was the most tight-lipped she'd ever been. She had an opinion about every subject and freely shared them with him and his brothers whenever possible. Her fire and intellect were just a couple of the things that challenged him and also what he loved about her. Her long blonde hair, lush lips, and perfect curves were icing on the cake. She was a knockout, and he was so proud to bring her back to Wilde.

"Son, why don't you introduce us to our new daughter-in-law?" Dad Bill grinned broadly. Mom stood between him and Dad Abe.

Jack took Carol's hand and placed it in his mother's. "Sweetheart, this is my mother, Ida Wilde, and these are my dads, her husbands, Bill and Abe."

Her mouth gaped open, then slammed shut. She shook his mother's hand. "Pleased to meet you, Mrs. Wilde."

"Call me 'mom,' child. We're family now." His mom's eyes sparkled with happy tears. "You've got your hands full with my boys. I can tell you that for sure. You need me to take the switch to their backsides, just let me know, hun."

Dad Bill kissed Carol's cheek. "The same goes for me, young lady."

"I think you'll handle them just fine, by the looks of you." Dad Abe kissed her other cheek. "But we are only a hop, skip, and a jump from any of their houses."

"Houses?" Carol asked.

"Yep. Our boys each built their own house." Dad Abe winked. "Your boys will do the same, and so will your grandsons."

"Abe, hush up. Let the girl settle in to being married first before you start pressuring her for grandchildren." His mother put her arm around Carol's shoulder. "Come with me. I think we women need a moment alone."

"Why?" Jack asked, not wanting to be away from his new bride a single second.

"Jack Wilde, you behave. I've finally gotten the daughter I always wanted. Let me have a few minutes with her. She might have some questions." Without another word, his mom led Carol to the secret, holy place the gentler gender enjoyed away from their men—the ladies' room.

* * * *

Carol faced the mirror in the ladies' room of the Wilde Community Center. She looked at her reflection and was stunned by how beautiful the bridal gown that she wore was.

How had the Wilde brothers put together an extravagant wedding on such short notice? And who really cared? After a month of the brothers sweeping her off her feet, had she just landed on her ass?

Mrs. Wilde stood behind her, grinning. "Hun, how you holding up?"

She blurted out, "Is everyone in Wilde crazy?"

Her new mother-in-law tilted her head to one side. "What do you mean?"

"You have two husbands."

The woman grinned. "And you have three."

"I'm so confused. I thought I was marrying Jack."

"Mmm. I'm sure there's a story about why you thought that, but let's delve into that later. First, do you love Jack?"

"Yes."

"And Tom?"

"I do," she confessed.

"Finally, what about Will? You love him, too?"

"Of course, but that doesn't change anything. What have I gotten myself into? I don't have a clue how to handle this. This kind of thing just isn't done."

Mrs. Wilde hugged her and whispered softly. "It is in Wilde. A woman can have it all. Lucky for you, child, you have three men that adore you."

Unable to hold back her emotions, Carol felt tears stream down her cheeks. "But I'm still a virgin."

"Sweet girl, you're just nervous." Mrs. Wilde nodded. "I understand now. You really are the daughter I always wanted. I know my boys, and they love you. I can see it in their eyes every time they look at you. They will be tender with you, trust me. You have nothing to fear, Carol."

* * * *

Jack watched his mother and his new wife come out of the ladies' room together. They were holding each other and smiling, which pleased him but also worried him a bit.

His brothers were standing next to him by the gift table. Most folks were leaving since this was the middle of the week and many of the husbands would be headed down the mine at seven in the morning.

"What do you think they were talking about alone?" Will asked.

Tom patted Jack and Will on the back. "I bet we're about to find out. Look at Mom. She's staring at us."

He was right about that. Jack had seen that look in his mother's eyes before, and it usually meant there was a lecture about to happen.

Sure enough, his mother led Carol to their dads, Bill and Abe, not

Jack and his brothers. Then his mom turned around and headed straight for them alone.

"Brace yourself, brothers. She's about to let us have it." Tom shook his head.

"What for?" Will asked.

"I guess we're about to find out," Jack stated.

Surprisingly, his mother didn't blast them, but instead said softly, "I'm so proud of you boys. I never doubted you would pick the right girl, but she is beyond my expectations as my new daughter-in-law."

Jack knew this was the calm before the storm. Mom always was tender before the big explosions. His commanders in Korea would've definitely benefited from sitting in her class about how to conduct a sneak attack.

Mom continued, "I already love this girl like my own daughter. If any of you boys ever hurt her, you won't only have my wrath to deal with, but you'll have your dads', too. Understand?"

"Yes, ma'am," they all said in unison.

"Boys, you know that this girl is inexperienced…in the bedroom."

Jack had already discussed that fact with Tom and Will. It had been very clear to all of them that Carol was a virgin. Sure, there had been heavy petting, but she had always stopped them when things got too hot. He'd actually known after only a week of being with her in San Francisco that she was the kind of woman he wanted to bring home to his parents.

"Well, are you going to answer me or not?"

Jack answered, "We know, Mom."

Tom and Will nodded

"You know she was a little confused about this wedding. I don't know why, but I'm sure you can put your three pointy heads together and figure it out."

Carol was confused? That explained so much about how she'd been acting. Why? They'd all asked her last night at dinner and she'd said yes. It just didn't make sense.

"Your dads and I raised you boys on how to treat a woman. I believe you've learned your lessons well, but now you have to prove it. Your bride is like a new rosebud just beginning to open up into full bloom. Promise me you will treat her with care."

"Mom, I love her." Jack was so pleased with how protective his mother was being for Carol. "Of course I will."

"I love her, too." Will hugged their mom. "I'll be good to her."

"I've never loved anyone like I love Carol, Mom." Tom kissed her on the cheek. "I would never do anything to hurt her."

"Look at my boys. You're all grown up and married." She smiled broadly. "You've made your mother proud. Let's go get your bride."

* * * *

Jack opened the front passenger door of Will's Cadillac for his new bride. She stepped out and gazed at his cabin, which he hadn't seen since shipping off to East Asia.

She'd changed clothes at the community center. Now, she wore a blue mid-length dress, which was tight enough to accentuate her gorgeous curves. The skirt portion hit below her knees and the top scooped low enough to show a temptingly scant amount of her cleavage. She wore black high heels that immediately drew his attention to her lovely legs.

Carol was shivering, likely from nerves, not from cold, since the air was warm outside. Still, he took off his jacket and placed it around her.

Her long eyelashes fluttered. She looked so beautiful.

"Thank you," she said. "I like how your place looks, Jack."

"That pleases me, honey," Jack said, and then he turned to Tom and Will. "Clearly, you guys took real good care of it while I was away. When did you add the front porch?"

"In March," Will said. "Hopefully it looks like the designs you sent to us."

"It's perfect." He'd missed being in Wilde, and now with his new wife by his side, he couldn't think of anywhere on earth he would rather be than home.

"Are those roses?" Carol asked.

"They are. Mom insisted I plant four bushes. All red. Told me it was important to spend as much time on the outside as I had on the inside. According to her, they made it more homey and appealing."

"I agree. Roses are my favorite flower, and red is my favorite color."

He smiled. "Mom knows best."

"Sweetheart, are you ready to go in?" Tom asked Carol.

She nodded.

Jack placed his arm around her shoulders, leading the way. When he got to the front steps, he lifted her up in his arms.

She gasped. "What are you doing, Jack?"

"It's tradition, sweetheart. A bride is supposed to be carried over the threshold. Or did I get that wrong?"

The smile that spread across her face pleased him. It was the first time she seemed to relax since the wedding.

"You're right, of course." She leaned her head into him and wrapped her arms around his neck.

He carried her into his cabin and gently lowered her down to her feet.

She looked around the main room. "This is amazing. You built this?"

"I did."

She walked over to the rock fireplace and touched the stone. "This, too?"

"All me, sweetheart," he confessed, proud of his work.

Will interjected, "You think this is something, wait until you see my place, honey."

She grinned and turned back to Jack. "It's so neat and orderly. I like that."

Tom cringed. Apparently, his brother's old messy habits hadn't changed while Jack had been away in Korea. He bet that Carol would get Tom in line. He could already see the impact she was having on Tom.

Everything here was just like Jack had left it before beginning his tour. Since there wasn't any dust, he knew his mother must've been there and given it the once-over to welcome him home.

Jack grabbed Carol's hand and squeezed. "But it definitely needs a woman's touch."

"So, is this where you want me to live?" she asked meekly.

Tom placed his arm around her waist. "You can choose here, my house, or Will's, for now. But we're going to build you a new house any way you wish."

Will nodded. "We want it to be your dream home."

"Would you like to see the rest of my place, sweetheart?" Jack asked.

"Yes, please."

He led her to the little kitchen, and she opened several cabinets. She was making herself at home, and that thrilled him.

Next, he showed her the back porch.

"Jack, this view is amazing."

He agreed. The mountains were beautifully lit by the full moon.

She sighed. "I bet this is a great place to enjoy coffee in the morning."

"It would be my pleasure to keep your cup full, honey." He would sit back there with her for as long as she liked. His dads had written him in Korea that once he got back to town, they wanted him working in the family business, the Wilde Silver Mine. But if Carol wanted a long breakfast on his back porch, he might be late to work every day.

"Baby, Jack might make great coffee, but you've got to try my waffles." Will winked. "They are out of this world."

"I would love that. May I see more?"

"Of course," Jack answered, pulling her in close to him.

They walked in, and he led her to the bedroom. He felt her begin to shiver.

"That's the biggest bed I've ever seen, Jack. It must be custom built."

"By my own hands." Jack looked at her emerald-green eyes. They were wider than he'd ever seen them before. She was nervous. He wanted to calm her fears. "Honey, I bet you'd like to freshen up."

She nodded, still trembling.

"The main bathroom is this way, sweetheart." Once they got to its door, he opened it up. Unlike the rest of his cabin, this was not like he'd left it when he'd shipped off last year. Sure, the fixtures were the same, including the big claw-foot tub he'd bought from Sears, Roebuck, but the plush towels, scented soaps and shampoos, perfumes, variety of candles, and the silky white negligee were all new. *More of Mom's handiwork.*

"Shouldn't you guys go first?" Carol asked.

"There's another bath where we can clean up," he told her. "We need no more than five minutes each. You can take all the time you need, sweetheart."

"Two bathrooms. That's quite extravagant for a cabin."

"I built this with you in mind, Carol."

"That's not possible." She shook her head. "You only met me a month ago."

He gently pressed his lips to hers, and heat flooded his body. "But I dreamed about you a long time ago, my love."

Her cheeks turned red, and she blinked several times.

He gazed at the most beautiful woman he'd ever laid eyes on—his new wife. "This is your night."

She whispered, "Thank you."

He walked into the hallway and shut the door behind him, allowing Carol time alone to get ready.

* * * *

Carol stood in the center of the bathroom, not sure what to do next. She scanned the room, which was lovely. Then she spotted an envelope on top of the towels. Her name was on it. She took the letter and opened it. It was from Ida, her new mother-in-law.

Dear Carol,

I hope you don't mind me being presumptuous, but I didn't think you would have time to pick a negligee out for yourself. I also wasn't sure what fragrances you would like, so I bought several. Hopefully one of these will be to your liking.

By the time you read this, we will have already met each other. I can't wait to get to know you and am certain we will become very close.

I know I will love you and you will make my boys very happy.
Ida

Carol felt tears brim in her eyes at the tenderness in Ida's note. Softly to herself, she said aloud, "I already love you, Mom."

Folding the letter carefully, she placed it back in the envelope. She would treasure Ida's letter for the rest of her life.

With a big sigh, she turned the two faucets of the beautiful claw-foot tub, allowing more hot water to flow than cold. She liked a very warm bath. Then it hit her that she'd forgotten something.

Turning around, her body rocked violently with a new set of shivers. Jack may have had her in mind when he built this room, but he'd forgotten one important item—the lock.

Carol recalled Ida's words in the ladies' room. "They will be tender with you, trust me. You have nothing to fear."

A wife had to trust her husband, and in her case—husbands. Before meeting the Wilde brothers, she hadn't even imagined such a thing was even possible. Legally, she was married to Jack, but in every other way that counted, she was married to all three of them.

She loved Jack's take-charge demeanor, Will's playful way, and Tom's serious side. And there was more about the men who had captured all her heart that she loved. They were kind, fun, caring, protective, and yes, very possessive. A month was short, but it had been long enough for her to fall head over heels for them.

She took off her shoes and slipped off her dress. Then she removed her hose and garter belt, looking back at the door with no lock. Trembles shook her as she realized there were three men just on the other side of that wooden door while she was standing on this side wearing only a slip, bra, and panties.

She knew in her heart they would never come through that door unless she called for them. Ida was right. The sweet woman's boys were tender and understanding.

Looking at the assortment of lotions and perfumes, she spotted her favorite fragrance—jasmine. She grabbed the bottle and put a few drops of the perfume into the warm water. The sweet fragrance wafted up in the steam, calming her nerves just a bit, knowing her husbands had told her in San Francisco how much they loved the scent.

Removing her undergarments, she tested the water with her toes. It was the perfect temperature. Then she lowered herself into the tub. The liquid warmth felt so good on her skin, but she continued to shiver. *How can I still be trembling in this hot water? Because I'm really nervous, that's why.*

She needed to get ahold of herself. She didn't want to disappoint her new husbands. She loved them, but had never been naked in front of any man before. She glanced over at the silky negligee and smiled, thankful Ida had bought it for her.

Again, she looked at the door, wondering what she would do if they suddenly came in. As a silly act of protection, she sunk down all the way below the water's surface until the top of her head was submerged. She smiled at how ridiculous she was being, and came up from the water.

She took the sponge, and started bathing.

A knock on the door startled her, and she slipped back down in the water to her chin. Her heart came alive in her chest, pounding hard and fast.

"Carol, do you need anything?" Will's voice came from the other side of the door.

"I'm fine. I'm just not ready yet. You're not coming in, are you?" Her voice sounded higher than normal.

"No, darlin'. Just checking on you. Take your time."

"Thank you." She listened intently to his retreating footsteps. Then she sighed.

After she was done bathing, she thought about getting out of the warm water and finishing getting ready, but then she decided to allow herself the pleasure of a short soak.

Closing her eyes, she slipped back down into the water. Submerging the sponge below the surface, she pulled it out and squeezed the water onto her body, imagining what it would feel like to have her men's hands touching her naked skin. She was filled with excitement but still terrified at what was to come.

She got out of the tub, knowing it was time to get over her fears and enjoy the evening with her husbands. Grabbing up one of the plush towels, she dried herself off slowly.

"Stop stalling, Carol," she said to herself. "Get on with it."

Quickly she grabbed the lotion and rubbed it onto her skin.

Another knock and she jumped.

"Yes?" She took the negligee and held it in front of her naked body. "Who is it?"

Will laughed. "One of your husbands, of course. I brought you a glass of wine, sweetheart."

She took a deep breath and cracked open the door just wide enough for her hand to grab the wine from him. Pulling the glass in, she shut the door. "Thank you, Will."

Without a thought, she downed the entire contents he'd brought her. The wine went down nice, warming her insides and calming her nerves.

Bolstering her courage, she slipped on the negligee. She took one of the brushes Ida had left for her and began brushing her hair, surprised at how dry it already was. *How long have I been in here?*

Gripping the side of the sink, she looked at her reflection in the mirror. Satisfied with what she saw, she took a really deep breath, held it, and then let it out slowly.

She opened the door and came face-to-face with her three wonderful husbands in nothing but robes.

* * * *

Will's jaw dropped at the sight of his bride standing in front of him and his two brothers. "My God, sweetheart, you look just like an angel."

He leaned forward and feathered his lips across hers. Taking her hand, he led her to the sofa by the rock fireplace in the main room. Jack sat down on one side of her and Tom on the other, just as they'd planned while she was bathing.

Will poured her another glass of wine. "Drink this, baby. It'll relax you."

In a single gulp, she drank down half of it before setting the glass down on the coffee table in front of her. "Thank you."

Sliding the wine bottle and her glass to the side, Will sat down on the table facing her. Then he touched her calves tenderly, enjoying the silkiness of her legs.

He watched Jack kiss her neck and Tom stroke her hair. She closed her eyes and sighed. He could feel the tension going out of her legs as she relaxed, brought on by their joint caresses and the wine she'd consumed.

Moving his hands up her legs until they were just under the bottom of her negligee, he felt a little tremble from her in his fingertips, which made his cock and balls throb.

He moved his hands further up her legs to her thighs until he almost touched her pussy. Leaning his head in close, he couldn't wait to taste her juices.

She was his world now, his everything. From the moment he'd met her, he knew that she was the one for him. Charming and sweet, sexy and smart, Carol was like no other woman he'd ever known before. "I love you, sweetheart."

"I love you, too, Will." Her words sent him to the moon.

* * * *

Tom threaded his fingers in Carol's soft tresses and kissed her on the cheek. With his free hand, he pulled the little strap down on her negligee, exposing her supple breast. Instantly, his cock lengthened under the robe he wore. Trailing soft kisses from her cheek to her shoulder, his lips landed lastly on her breast. When he placed his lips on her nipple, he felt it grow taut. Unable to resist, he lightly bit her bud and was rewarded when she leaned her body into him.

He'd always seen life as black and white. Humor normally escaped Tom, but Carol's wit mesmerized him. She helped him see a whole world of colors and possibilities. She amazed him with her cute smile and contagious giggle. His new bride was more than he'd ever dreamed possible, and he relished the future they would spend together.

"I love you," he whispered in her ear.

"I love you too, Tom."

He gently bit her nipple again, and she began to pant. Out of the corner of his eye, he saw Will lick her pussy, causing her to tremble more. Opposite where he sat, Jack was sucking on her other breast.

"Oh my God, what's happening to me?" There was a mix of panic and passion in her tone.

"Sweetheart, let go and enjoy the pleasure we're giving you. Let your body respond to our touches."

She shook from head to toe, and her hands landed on the back of Will's head. Her panting and writhing came faster and faster.

Tom sucked on her breast like a man dying of thirst, and his balls grew heavy.

When she gasped, he knew she'd climaxed, and that pleased him beyond measure.

* * * *

After Carol's orgasm subsided a bit, Jack stood, guiding her to her feet with his hands. Tom and Will pulled her negligee to the floor. He saw her lips tremble a bit.

"My God, you're beautiful." Jack lifted her up into his arms. Then he carried her into the bedroom with Will and Tom following behind.

Placing her in the middle of the bed, he gazed down at his new wife. She was gorgeous. "Sweetheart, I love you so much."

He took off his robe and crawled on top of her sexy body. Tom and Will also removed their robes and got on the bed on opposite sides of her. It was time to claim Carol, to make her his—both in body and soul. "This may hurt you a little bit, baby."

Without another word, he guided the head of his cock into her pussy.

Her eyes went wide, and he felt her tighten around his dick.

"Easy, darlin'. There's no rush."

Tom tenderly kissed her cheek while Will stroked her hair and rubbed her neck.

As he slowly pushed his dick in deeper, he felt her barrier. "Now take a deep breath, sweetheart."

* * * *

Carol obeyed, filling her lungs to the max. Then she felt an instant searing pain as Jack pierced her virgin flesh, causing her to release her breath.

Her passion exploded, washing away the sting quickly. As he went deeper inside her, she wrapped her legs around his waist. When he started rhythmically going in and out of her body, her desire took over and her hips began to move, matching his every stroke.

A deluge of need she'd never known possible filled her. With her hands on his shoulders, she raked his skin with her fingernails.

In a heated whisper, she confessed, "Jack, I love you so much."

He kissed her deeply, expanding her desire for him.

Moving faster and faster, Jack was pushing her to the brink. Her body seemed to have a mind of its own, as her insides clenched down on his cock, again and again. She felt warmth and overpowering sensations throughout all her body, inside and out.

Her back arched off the mattress, as Jack filled her with one powerful, lasting thrust. She screamed, feeling tears of pleasure stream down her cheeks. Vibrations rolled through her, igniting all her nerve endings, and she began to shiver uncontrollably.

Her husbands gently massaged, kissed, and touched her as the orgasm they'd given her continued to undulate through her body. The feeling seemed to last forever.

When her climax softened to a glow, Will lifted her off the bed and into his arms. Hoping she had pleased her three men, Carol whispered, "Did I...well, was everything...okay?"

Will gazed down at her, causing her another little tremble. "Darlin', you were amazing."

She saw Jack and Tom stripping the bed as Will carried her out of the bedroom and into the bathroom. Will lowered her onto the toilet seat.

Placing the stopper in the drain, he turned on the water to fill the tub. "Honey, you like your bath really warm, right?"

She nodded.

He made a couple of turns on the faucets and then came back to her. He cupped her chin and leaned down and kissed her tenderly. Now, she had no qualms that they were both naked in front of each other. In fact, it felt so natural to her.

Tom, also still naked, came in with a full glass of wine and handed it to her. "Baby, this is for you."

"Thank you." She took a little sip and glanced at the steam rising from the bathtub.

Tom stroked her hair. "How are you feeling?"

"Wonderful." She set down her glass. "And a bath is exactly what I need right now. Time for me to get into that watery oasis, fellows."

Will shook his head. "No you don't, Carol."

Confused, she asked, "What do you mean?"

"You're exhausted." He lifted her again into his arms.

"I can walk, Will."

He grinned. "Sweetheart, let your husbands take care of you tonight."

"Okay," she said, feeling like a princess.

Will lowered her into the bath. Immediately, her body began to relax in the warm water. He sat on the edge of the tub on one side and Tom sat on the other. Each had a sponge that they plunged below the water's surface.

Will pressed his hot mouth to her waiting lips. A shiver rolled through her, despite the warm water. Tom washed her legs with his soapy sponge. Will worked on her shoulders with his. Her lips began to tremble slightly. She sighed and closed her eyes, letting herself relish being bathed by Tom and Will.

Tom moved up her legs. "How does this feel, baby?"

"Good. Really good."

When the sponge in his hand pressed against her sex, she moaned softly. Will moved his sponge to her breasts, sending new heat between her legs. Her men washed every inch of her body, igniting a craving inside her. Tom, Will, and Jack had been so tender and patient with her. Now, she wanted more, needed more.

Tom and Will lifted her out of the water. After placing her on her feet, they began drying her with the plush, soft towels. Wearing his robe, Jack came in the bathroom carrying her negligee and some slippers in one hand and his brothers' robes in the other.

"Hi, sweetheart," Jack said, handing Tom and Will their robes. "You must be famished. Thankfully, someone stocked the kitchen and fridge for us. I've got some fruit, cheese, and crackers ready for you on the back porch. Do you like hot tea?"

"That sounds so refreshing."

"Let's get you dressed." Jack stepped in front of her, lifting the negligee over her head. The silky garment fell softly down her body. Then he put the comfy slippers on her feet.

"Hey, there's a bit of a chill in the air tonight." Will put his arm around her shoulders. "We need to get our lovely bride a robe before we take her outside."

Tom grinned. "There's only one robe that I can think of that will fit her."

"I bet you're right, Tom." Will laughed. "Jack, you still have that robe Mom made for you?"

Jack shook his head. "How would I know? I've been in Korea for a year."

"Now, I'm curious," she said, noticing the mischievous smirks from Tom and Will and Jack's obvious unease on the topic of the mysterious robe.

"Best to show you first, baby. I know right where it is." Tom walked out of the bathroom.

"Jack, tell me about this robe of yours," she asked.

His eyebrows shot up. "Honey, you've got to understand that I was just a kid. Will and Tom love picking on me since I'm the youngest of the three of us."

Will snorted, "Mom always loved spoiling him, honey. Besides, you never got rid of it, Jack, did you?"

Tom was back and holding Jack's boyhood robe in his left hand.

At first, Carol didn't see what the hubbub was all about. "What's that sewed onto the shoulders?"

Will and Tom burst into laughter. Then Tom turned the robe around. Carol giggled at the sight of the red cape with the gold capital "S" attached to the white robe.

Jack just stood there, shaking his head.

"Come on, brother. Say it for us," Tom teased. "Faster than a…what?"

Will added, "More powerful than a—"

"Shut up, guys," Jack said with a chuckle. "Just put it on Carol and let's get her some food."

Tom placed the robe around her and picked her up into his arms.

"If you guys keep carrying me around everywhere, I'm going to forget how to walk. After all, with this robe, I bet I can fly to the porch."

They all laughed as Tom led the way to the back of the cabin with her in his arms. Once they were out on the back porch, Tom sat her down in one of the wooden chairs.

The goodies Jack had put together were delicious. The cup of tea tasted wonderful, and it warmed her insides.

She and her three husbands sat in silence for a bit, enjoying each other's presence and the world around them.

She gazed up into the cloudless night sky filled with millions of stars. When a bright streak shot across the blackness, she gasped. Pointing, she said, "Look, a falling star."

"Hurry up, sweetheart. Make a wish." Jack took her hand and squeezed.

She hadn't seen such beauty in the sky since viewing the northern lights one early-spring night during her childhood in Maine. Closing her eyes, she made her wish.

"What did you wish for, baby?" Tom asked.

She shook her head. "If I told you, that would ruin the magic."

"So that's how you're going to play this." His mouth curved up into a wicked grin. "Well, I think it's time to show you a little more magic, sweetheart." Then he lifted her back up into his arms.

She hoped they were going to make love to her again. She'd never expected her body could experience such glorious feelings. She wanted to learn more and more about the bedroom, both for her own pleasure and for the pleasure of her husbands.

Tom carried her back into the bedroom. Jack had remade the bed and it looked so inviting to her.

Gently, Tom lowered her facedown onto the soft blankets and pillows. "Time for your next lesson, baby."

Though she was unsure what was coming next, anticipation overwhelmed her. Her cravings for the sensations they'd given her earlier drove her mad.

Tom crawled onto the bed next to her. His hands drifted lightly down her back, raising goose bumps on her skin. Jack got on the other side of her and began stroking her hair. She felt Will position himself between her legs, pushing his fingers up and deeply through her sex. Her husbands' intimate touches incited a hundred hot vibrations inside her.

She felt Tom apply something slick to her backside, which puzzled but also aroused her. Odd, but true.

Turning her head to the side, she came face-to-face with Jack. He smiled and plastered his full lips to her mouth just as Tom pierced her tightness back there with his finger. The pain was tolerable, especially since it gave birth to something stronger and more powerful— unabashed desire.

Will continued pressing her sex with his hand, making her even wetter than before. "I can't wait to have you, love. I want to fill you up with my cock."

His words ignited a firestorm inside her. Crazed and so very hot, she began to pant.

Jack stroked her chin. "We're all here for you, Carol. This is all for you." As he licked her neck, she felt the heat in her cheeks explode.

Tom continued to manipulate her ass, sending another finger inside her. His handling of her backside expanded her need for more from her husbands, her need to have them inside her body once again.

Jack reached between the mattress and her chest, and she felt him capture her nipple with his thumb and forefinger. When he pinched her tiny bit of flesh, she moaned, licking her lips.

"You're all I could've ever dreamed of, darlin'." Will applied the perfect torture to her clitoris with his hand, making her deliciously dizzy.

She felt Tom crawl on top of her, pinning her body with his entire weight. The tip of his dick touched her anus, making her shiver. Realization of what he was about to do caused her to hold her breath, though she was willing to surrender everything to him, to all of them.

"Baby, keep breathing," Tom instructed.

"I'm trying," she choked out.

He kissed her neck and whispered, "Trust me, Carol. This will give you pleasure."

His words softened her anxiety just a bit, and she was able to breathe more deeply.

"That's my baby. In and out. Really slow."

Inhaling deeper than before, she felt her desire for him to claim her in this unusual way grow. She'd never thought about sex in this fashion, but being possessed by Tom this way was something she wanted, needed, craved. As she exhaled, Tom pushed his cock past her tightness and into her backside. The sting was intense but tolerable. She chewed on her lip and fisted the sheets, fighting back the pain. In no time, the ache turned into something hot, extreme, and fierce. Her passions were alive and well and exploding inside her body.

Tom thrust further into her ass, and her womb began to clench. Without a word, he rolled over, pulling her along with him, keeping his cock seated inside her ass, until her back rested on his front and her front faced the ceiling.

She looked up at Jack and Will, gazing down at her with apparent awe. Will moved onto the bed and got on top of her, positioning his dick until it pressed on her pussy, which was soaked from passion.

"Please," she begged, unable to hold back her desire any longer. "Please, Will. Take me."

He kissed her and pushed his cock into her channel. She'd never felt so taken over in all her life as her two husbands filled her completely. They began to pump their dicks in and out of her body, one from behind and the other in the front, and she closed her eyes tight, mentally holding on for the ride of her life.

She was sandwiched between these two men, her husbands. The thought sent her into the stratosphere, and more sensations shot through her.

She felt Jack touch her cheek. "I want to feel your pretty mouth around my cock, sweetheart."

Opening her eyes, she found his erect dick only a fraction of an inch from her lips. He'd moved himself onto the bed to feed her his cock. She stuck out her tongue and tasted the salty drop glistening on the slit of his dick.

"Yes, darlin'. Perfect," Jack said.

His encouragement spurred her on, and she opened her mouth as wide as she could. Pleasing her husbands was all she wanted, and her reward would be ultimate pleasure.

Jack leaned into her and gently sent his cock past her lips. Twirling her tongue around the head of his dick, she cupped her hand around his beefy balls.

"Wow," Jack growled. "That feels great, honey."

She sent her other hand around Will's neck and her legs around his waist.

Tom and Will continued thrusting into her, driving her to the very edge of insanity.

Sucking hard on Jack's dick, her body began writhing between her three husbands, as if it had a mind of its own.

Everything—Tom claiming her ass, Will filling her pussy, Jack possessing her mouth—mixed together into a brew of hot, unimaginable pleasure. It was as if her entire life had led her to this very moment—her wedding night.

Will's eyes closed tight. "I'm coming."

She felt his cock pulse inside her, and her womb clenched tight around him, accepting his seed.

Jack cupped the back of her neck. "Drink all of me, sweetheart."

She swallowed every drop of him.

Tom thrust into her ass and came inside her, too.

With every beat of her heart, another detonation of wild, climactic sensations came alive inside her. What to call the things they'd imparted to her this night? Wondrous joy. *Überwältigende liebe. La petite mort.*

Though she spoke English, German, and a little French, there weren't words that could describe what Tom, Will, and Jack had given her.

None of them moved for a little bit. She was glad to be surrounded by her guys.

As her breathing and heartbeat slowed, Will and Jack moved off the bed. Tom kept his arms wrapped around her from behind.

Jack leaned down and kissed her again. "I love you, my wife."

"I love you, my husband."

Will also kissed her. "Love you, honey."

"I love you, Will."

Tom rolled her onto her side, and then swung his legs off the bed. Next, he lifted her up into his arms.

"What now, Tom?" she asked.

"A little refreshing shower, sweetheart."

"You guys must be the cleanest cowboys in Nevada. You realize this will be my third washing tonight?"

"We do, but this one is special, love," Tom said.

He carried her into the bathroom with the shower that they'd gotten ready in while she had taken her bath. Since it was large enough for all of them, she easily stood in the middle of her three fellows.

One at a time, her husbands went under the showerhead, soaking their muscled bodies. Though they didn't ask for her help, she wanted to wash them, just like they'd done for her. Taking one of the cloths hanging from the rod on the wall, she put it under the shower's stream, getting it nice and wet. After adding soap to the cloth, she placed it on Jack's muscled chest first.

His cock lengthened, and she giggled, reaching out to squeeze him. "I have quite an effect on you, cowboy."

"You bet your ass you do, sweetheart."

She turned to Will, and instead of washing his chest first, she went straight for his dick.

He smiled, and she felt his shaft grow under the cloth. "Me, too, doll. Me, too."

Getting up on her tiptoes, she kissed him. Turning to Tom, she saw he was already aroused.

Tom's voice rumbled deep in his chest. "My turn, baby."

He lifted her up as if she was a feather, and then he slid her down until his hard cock entered her sex. She wrapped her legs around his waist and her arms around his neck. With brute strength, he gently lifted her up and down, sending his dick deep into her body. There was determination in his piercing eyes, his rhythmic movements, and his hot breaths. He thrust into her again and again, sending her quickly into a state of euphoria filled with tingles and shivers. Then he shot his seed deep inside her.

She raked her nails on his shoulders.

Totally spent, she melted into his body. As her three new husbands helped her back into bed, she sighed with contentment before drifting off to sleep.

* * * *

The dew sparkled on the trees like little diamonds and birds sang from every branch. The mountains off in the distance looked so majestic. Northern Nevada was quite beautiful. Living here was going to be wonderful.

Enjoying the gorgeous morning, Carol sat on the back porch sipping the fresh cup of coffee Jack had just poured her.

Tom sat by her. Though he was reading the newspaper, he also held her hand.

Jack sat on the other side of her, sipping his own cup of coffee. His eyes never left her, which made her smile.

"Maybe you should take a picture, Jack. It'll last longer."

"Sweetheart, I plan on taking lots of pictures of you. Hell, I might even take up painting. Here you are, right in front of me—perfection."

Even though she loved hearing him say that, she replied, "I'm absolutely not, and you will soon see that fact after I've been around longer."

"We could argue about this all day. You're never going to change my mind, honey."

She shook her head and smiled.

Will came out of the cabin, balancing several plates of hot waffles. The aroma of the breakfast he'd made for all of them was wonderful.

"Darlin', I hope you enjoy this," Will said, placing Carol's plate in front of her on the table and handing her a fork.

"If the mouthwatering smell is any indication, I'm sure I am going to love it." She looked down at the simple white plate, filled with a golden-brown waffle covered in maple syrup and a generous amount of fresh butter. Two crispy strips of thick bacon sat on the rim of the dish. The breakfast he'd whipped up for her was ideal.

Tom put down the newspaper and took his plate. Jack set his cup down and took his. Will sat across from her, and they all began to eat.

Will's food was just as good as she thought it would be.

After they finished the meal, Jack poured them all more coffee.

"Honey, Mom told us you were confused about the wedding." Jack rubbed her back. "Didn't we make it clear to you in San Francisco?"

"You probably did, Jack, but I was battling a sinus infection. My ears were stopped up. I got a shot before we went out that night, but it didn't really kick in fully until the next morning. I knew you were asking me to marry you, but after that things got real fuzzy. When I think back, I now realize that Tom and Will were asking me, too."

He leaned in and kissed her. "I'm sorry, honey. We didn't know."

Tom stroked her hair. "Are you okay with being married to me, too?"

"And me?" Will asked, also, taking both her hands in his and squeezing them gently.

"More than okay. I fell in love with all three of you in San Francisco, but I thought I would have to choose. I never knew this kind of family existed. I didn't know a woman could fall in love with more than one man. Your mom helped me understand a woman's heart. There is room for more than one love. I'm so glad I didn't have to choose, but I do have some questions for you."

"Ask away, doll," Will said.

"First, what about children?"

Jack answered, "Of course, we want children, honey. We'd love to have a houseful."

She shook her head. "No. That's not what I mean. Last night was amazing. I never dreamed it would be like that. But I could be pregnant. How will I know who the father is?"

Tom spoke first. "God, I hope you are, baby. And if you are, that child would have three fathers."

Made sense to her and also took away any worry inside her.

"Of course you wouldn't have known that, sweetheart. You're not from Wilde." Jack kissed her on the cheek.

"How did this all get started? This is so unusual."

Tom began the tale in his typical serious manner. "Our family came here in the eighteen hundreds and discovered the silver mine. The town grew up around it. Our ancestors had seen so many towns go bust when other mines were divided between heirs. They didn't want the same thing to happen to our town."

"So, they didn't want to split the ownership of the mine?" Glad to learn more about her new home, she asked, "That's how the plural marriage thing got started?"

Tom sounded like a professor to her as he continued to recount the history of Wilde. "That and there were few women around. From the beginning, living in plural marriages has been the standard for our family. The citizens supported our practice since it kept the town and the mine thriving. Though not everyone lives our kind of life. Most families in Wilde choose our way."

She nodded. "I can understand why."

Jack's eyebrows shot up. "You can?"

"Oh yes, Jack. I'm one woman who has three wonderful husbands who love me and I love them. Though I was confused about things last night, I'm clear as can be today. I choose all three of you, now and for the rest of my life."

"Sweetheart, you've made us all so very happy," Jack said.

"One more question."

Her guys leaned forward, apparently hanging on her every word.

She smiled and said, "I want to teach. Is there a high school in Wilde?"

They all nodded.

Together, her husbands lifted her up and took her back into the cabin. Her insides began to tingle, as anticipation for more of their lovemaking filled her with excitement.

* * * *

Wilde, Nevada – May 1981

Carol Wilde sat at her kitchen table in her home, the house her three wonderful husbands had built for her nearly thirty years ago, enjoying the company of Mary, her beautiful daughter-in-law, and her gorgeous new grandson, who was beginning to stir.

Anxiously, Mary said, "I think he might be hungry or dirty. I just don't know, Mom."

"Give Austin to me, hun." Pushing her students' yet-to-be-graded homework to the side, Carol reached for the bundle of joy that had come into her family just three days ago. "You'll get the hang of this fast. You still have your training wheels on. I know I had my hands full with Daniel those first few days. By this time next week, you'll be a pro."

"You don't know how much that means to me." Mary wiped a tear from her eye. "You've always been there for me, Mom. You remember giving me your letter on my wedding night?"

Carol nodded, dotting kisses on Austin's sweet face.

Like her, Mary had come to Wilde with no idea how things worked in the tiny mining town. She'd tried to be there for the young woman just like her own mother-in-law, Ida, had been for her all those years ago.

"Every time I get stressed or overwhelmed, like now, I read yours and Mama Ida's." Mary reached in her purse and brought out the two letters.

Carol smiled. "So like me. I kept my letter from Ida in my purse, too."

"Do you mind if I read yours, Mom?"

"Of course not. I'm so glad it means so much to you, Mary."

Dear Mary,
When I first came to Wilde and married my three wonderful husbands, I was so nervous, I was afraid to come out of the bathroom.

Then I found a note from my new mother-in-law.

As you probably noticed, I included her letter with mine. I've kept it all these years to continually remind me of her gracious love to a girl she barely knew but already welcomed into her family.

I want you to know that I feel the same way about you.

You have given me such joy and happiness already.

You are my daughter now and forever, and I will always be there for you in any capacity you might need.

My sons love you so much, sweetheart, and I know your life with them will be amazing.

Someday you may enjoy the pleasure of having a new daughter in your life and will also feel the need to write her a letter. Please enclose Ida's and mine with yours. Not only will we start a tradition, but your new daughter-in-law will see just how wonderful our life is in Wilde.

Love you, Mom

Mary ended her reading by wiping her eyes. "I love you, Mom."

Carol held Austin with one arm and had to wipe her eyes with the other. "I love you, daughter."

"Would you like me to read Momma Ida's to you, too?"

"Don't you dare, Mary. I'm already a mess." God, she missed Ida.

Her mother-in-law had outlived Dad Bill and Dad Abe, her two husbands, by a couple of years. There had been sadness in Momma Ida's eyes that she had spotted from time to time after their deaths, but the amazing woman had never let on to anyone, especially her sons. Momma Ida had never failed to tell her how fulfilled life had been for her in Wilde.

Last spring, Momma Ida had died peacefully in her sleep with Carol at her bedside. She'd been a friend, a confidant, and a mother to Carol until her very last breath.

The baby settled down and closed his eyes, which pleased her very much. In another month, she would say good-bye to her last class at Wilde High School. Teaching biology for all these years had been amazing, but it was time to retire.

"So you say Daniel was a handful. What about Craig and Dillon?" Mary asked. "I bet they were trouble."

"They're your husbands, child. You ought to know."

"Speaking of your sons, I have a problem, Mom. I can't walk into a room without one or all of them slapping me on my butt. I know they're only playing but sometimes it really smarts."

Carol laughed as old memories bubbled up in her. "Hun, there's something about these Wilde men that a woman has to stay a couple of steps ahead of them. Tom, Will, and Jack did the same thing to me for nearly an entire year after we moved into this house. They'd come in from work and I'd have dinner on the table and they would each slap my ass. This happened every night. I wouldn't have minded if they would've kept that kind of thing for the bedroom instead of the kitchen."

"Mom, you naughty girl."

She smiled, and said teasingly, "Naughty and nice, child. Just like you."

Mary blushed, making her face appear even more beautiful. "How did you get them to stop?"

"One night I put on the biggest pair of slacks I owned. Then I took a solid oak board and positioned it just so in my pants."

"You mean—?"

"One at a time, they each came in and did their usual slap on my butt. Hurt their hands just enough to make my point. You should've heard Jack. He actually asked me if I had started working out. It was priceless. They never stopped, but their hard slaps became gentle pats. Well, at least in the kitchen."

They both fell into a fit of laughter. The baby whined a bit, and they bit back their chuckles. Austin's three granddads and three dads came frantically running into the kitchen.

Her eldest son Daniel spoke first. "Is the baby all right? We heard a commotion."

Carol smiled, gazing down at Austin, who was already drifting back to sleep. "We're just fine, son."

Tom, Will, and Jack came up behind her, gazing at their new grandchild. Their pride was easy to see.

Tom kissed her cheek. "Sweetheart, our grandson is something, isn't he?"

"Yes, he is."

Jack stroked her hair. "He's got Daniel's eyes, darlin'. Your eyes."

She grinned. "And Craig's nose, sweetheart. Your nose."

They all laughed.

Will rubbed her shoulders. "But he's a gorgeous baby, just like our daughter-in-law. Don't you agree, honey?"

"He is beautiful, just like Mary." She nodded, recalling so many memories since her wedding night.

Her three amazing men—Jack, Tom, and Will—had given her so much it was impossible to even measure or put into words. And having her three boys had multiplied her joy on top of that. In her new role as a grandmother, she would enter the next chapter of her wonderful life in Wilde, Nevada.

* * * *

Wilde, Nevada – Present

Sipping his sweet iced tea, Pappy Jack sat on his porch watching his kids getting ready for another barbeque.

God how these children love to eat, especially when they get to fire up the ol' grill.

His three sons had caught themselves quite the woman in Mary. Daniel, Craig, and Dillon were new granddads and doing a fine job of it, too. Per usual, his boys were surrounding the smoking meat, arguing over who was the better grill master.

"Pappy Jack, would you like some company?" Jesse, his granddaughter-in-law asked, holding the reason for today's celebration in her arms.

"You bet I do. Bring that baby up here to me, young lady."

The new mother smiled and came up on the porch, sitting next to him and in Carol's chair. She handed over the precious bundle to him.

"My grandsons helping you out with this little one or do I need to take a switch to their behinds?"

"They are, Pappy Jack. Jackson has taken over all the housework. You know what a great chef Phoenix is. He's doing all the cooking. Dallas does the laundry, and Denver handles all the shopping."

"And Austin?" He looked over at his five grandsons who were helping Mary pull out the picnic tables. God, he was so proud of them.

"He demands I sleep, so he always takes the night shift with this one." Jesse leaned over and kissed her baby on the forehead.

"Sounds just like Austin to me," he told her.

Jesse placed her hand on his forearm. "Sounds like most of you Wilde men to me."

It was always so much fun having all the kids here. They made his life complete and fulfilled. "Wilde, Nevada, is quite the change from where you came from, Jesse. Most outsiders don't make it here, but you sure have."

"I didn't at first. But your grandsons captured my heart and so did the town. I had to learn to fit in. Plus, Mary gave me some letters on my wedding day that helped me do just that. One was from your mother, Ida. Another was—"

"Jesse, I know about the letters you women share with one another on the day you get married. A secret tradition that isn't so secret, is it?"

"What do you mean, Pappy Jack?"

"You've shown them to my grandsons, haven't you?"

She smiled. "Not on our wedding night, but later, yes."

"That's also part of the tradition, sweetheart."

"Mary's letter meant the world to me. And though I never knew Grandma Ida or Grandma Carol, they are a part of my heart."

"Carol would've loved you, Jesse. You're a lot like her. I remember that first day I met you and you were soaked from the rain. You and Dallas came here. The only clothes I had to give you were hers. I love you, granddaughter."

"I love you, Pappy Jack." She kissed him on the cheek. The baby started to cry. "I'll take that handful back from you now. Diaper changing time."

"This old man has changed many a diaper in his day. Do you mind?"

"Of course not." Jesse stood. "That'll give me a chance to help Momma Mary get things set up. I put the diaper bag back in the bedroom."

He carried his grandchild into the cabin. "Just like old times, little one."

Once in the bedroom and onto the task at hand, he thought about how rich and awesome his life had been.

Awesome. That was a word he didn't hear when he was young, but it sure was appropriate now.

Carol's spunk had never lessened in or out of this bedroom, helping to keep a constant smile on his face.

Now, old goat, don't go into that. He grinned at his own thoughts.

"You've got your whole life in front of you," he told his grandchild, who was cooing sweetly. "You're going to have some wonderful adventures and amazing moments. Still, some days are going to be hard, but you're a Wilde. We get through them."

The darkest times for him and Carol had been the losses of Tom and Will. Of course it had been difficult after the many years they'd all had together. Tom had been the first to pass, and he and Will had taken it hard, but Carol had been grief stricken.

Tom's death had been so unexpected. He'd left early in the morning to mend some broken fences. When he hadn't returned by lunchtime, Carol had gotten to worrying. He and Will had gone to look for him and found Tom on the ground. He'd suffered a major heart attack. It had taken him and Will over a month to get a smile out of their wife, but like Jack had always known about Carol—she was tough.

"You've got your great-grandma's eyes," he said, kissing the baby on the cheek. "She would've squeezed the daylights out of you."

Carol's smiles, though genuine, hadn't been as bright and warm as before Tom's death. On more than one occasion, he and Will had found her crying. Whenever they did, she'd wipe her eyes, claiming allergies or some other silly excuse had been the cause. But both he and Will saw through her pretense, as they, too, carried a hole in their hearts left by Tom's absence.

That was my Carol, not wanting to upset anyone. God, I loved that woman.

"Has your momma told you about her letters? She will one day." The baby's tiny finger wrapped around his ancient, crooked thumb. "I have my own letter, but let's keep that secret between you and me."

Actually, he had boxes and boxes of notes and letters from Carol, but the last one she'd written to him was the most special. She'd made sure he wouldn't find it until after she was gone, placing it in her nightstand drawer.

Dear Jack,

When you find this letter, I will already be gone. I want to tell you not to be sad, but you and I both know that's a part of the healing. When we lost Tom, I thought I would die, but I had you and Will to help me through it. After Will passed, you and I clung to each other.

Please let our boys and our sweet daughter Mary help you through the dark times you must face. They'll need you as much as you'll need them.

It breaks my heart to leave you, my love. I wish I could stay. I want to see more sunrises with you on our porch more than anything. But we both have learned long ago that death is a part of life. And what a life you've given me. So many good years. From the very first time I met you, Tom, and Will in San Francisco, until now has been an adventure. I wouldn't change a single second.

I love you with all my heart, Jack.

Until we meet again,

All my love,

Your Carol

"I wish I could be there for your wedding, your new babies, your adventures," he said, lifting his grandchild into his arms. "You've got to be the cutest granddaughter in the world." Jack kissed the baby once again. "Let's go see our family, little Carol."

THE END

WWW.CHLOELANG.COM

SIREN
Publishing

Wilde, Nevada 3

Ménage Everlasting

Her Two Wilde
Billionaire
Bad Boys

Chloe Lang

THE
BDSM
collection

HER TWO WILDE BILLIONAIRE BAD BOYS

Wilde, Nevada 3

CHLOE LANG
Copyright © 2014

Chapter One

Leaving the diner, Danielle Glass walked down Main Street to the sheriff's office. She wondered why Sheriff Wayne Champion had summoned her. It certainly couldn't be to give her statement again.

With all her being, she wanted to forget what had happened to her in Malcolm Winters's basement.

She stopped in her tracks and closed her eyes, recalling the horror she'd experienced at the hands of the beast.

Thank God, the bastard is dead. Even though the psycho was gone, her nightmares remained, mingling with older, dark memories.

Wyatt and Wade Masters, Mackenzie's men, had taken out the son of a bitch and saved Danielle and Mac's brother, Trent, from certain death. Mackenzie was a strong woman, and like her, was not native to Wilde, Nevada.

Wilde was different on so many levels, but the one thing that had made it the perfect place for Danielle to stay was that the citizens welcomed everyone without question. Questions were the last thing she needed. Being invisible and off the radar was the most important thing to her.

Turning left on Coyote Street, she headed to the entrance of the jailhouse.

She walked in and found the sheriff talking on the phone.

He motioned for her to take a seat. "She's here now."

She tensed. *Who's he talking to about me?*

"Thanks, Austin." The sheriff hung up the phone.

Realizing the man on the other end of the phone had been Austin Wilde, she breathed a sigh of relief. Austin was married to Jessie, one of the women Danielle had grown close to.

"Thanks for coming, Danielle."

"What's this about, Sheriff? I really have told you everything I can about what happened with Winters. I don't have anything to add."

"I know, but this isn't about that. Not exactly. I have two reasons for calling you in."

She didn't like the sound of that.

"You know that Austin and I have been working together to bring down the drug cartel that Winters was working for."

"Yes."

"Austin found out that some of the cartel's known associates have been digging around and asking questions about you and Trent Green. We believe that they are under the assumption that you and Trent have the money that Malcolm stole from them."

"That doesn't make any sense. We were Winters's prisoners, not his partners."

Sheriff Champion shrugged. "The cartel's rationale isn't something anyone can understand, least of all me. Likely, they think Malcolm bragged to you and Trent about the four hundred thousand dollars he'd stolen from them. In their eyes, why wouldn't he? Winters planned on killing you."

"And we would've been dead if the Masters hadn't shown up when they did."

"That's true," he said. "I want you to be careful, Danielle. There's been no sign of the cartel in Wilde, but I'd like to assign a bodyguard to you."

"I'm fine, Sheriff. I can take care of myself." *I've been doing it my whole life.*

"I'm worried about you."

"I appreciate your concern, but I have a gun of my own."

"Most in Wilde do." He grinned. "This might be the best armed town in all of America."

"Sheriff, I really don't want some man following me around town like a puppy dog. I promise to keep my eyes open. If you and Austin get wind of someone from the cartel coming to town, I will reconsider your offer."

"That's just it, Danielle. We don't know when they might be coming. Better to have the drop on them before they have the drop on us, if you get my meaning." He leaned forward. "Which brings me to my next reason for having you come here. I did a little digging myself on you and Trent."

Her heart skipped a beat. "What for?"

"I know you aren't who you say you are, Danielle. Why?"

She closed her eyes. Wilde had been the longest stop for her since turning twelve. The year before coming here, she'd lived in three different cities. The year before that, five. She'd even started imagining that she would be able to stay for good. Not possible. Not now.

"Danielle, I want to help." The sheriff was a very kind man.

She opened her eyes and looked at the sheriff. Wayne Champion was like the dad she'd never had. His sons, all pillars in Wilde, adored him. For the first time in her life, she knew she'd found a man she could trust.

Taking a deep breath, she began. "My real name is Danielle Roberson. I ran away from home when I was twelve."

She told him everything—every horrific detail of why she kept her real identity secret. Tears rolled down her cheeks as the memories flooded out of her.

He came around his desk and pulled her into an embrace.

"Sweetheart, I understand. Don't worry. Everything is going to be okay. I'll see to it."

"Please, Sheriff. Don't tell anyone. I don't want my family to find me. Ever."

"I won't. Your secret is safe with me."

* * * *

Just as the jet hit some turbulence, Lance Archer threw the football to his friend and he stumbled back to his seat.

Their pilot's voice came over the speaker. "Sorry, sirs."

"No worries." Chuck, still on his feet, held the football they'd been tossing to each other during the flight. "When will we be landing?"

"Another hour, Mr. Covington. I would suggest you buckle in. I'm expecting it to be a bumpy ride from here on."

"How many times do I have to tell you, Lyle, not to call him 'Mr. Covington.'" Lance always enjoyed a chance to tease. "Call him *Chuck.*"

"Yes, sir, Mr. Archer."

"Don't you dare, Lyle," Chuck said firmly. "There's only one person in the world that gets away with that."

Their pilot of the past five years laughed. "I know, sir. I know. I'll let you know when we are ten minutes from approach."

"Thanks." Lance turned to his best friend in the world. "Great catch during the turbulence, bro. Toss it over."

Chuck lobbed the ball to him. "Buddy, you've got to stop trying to get everyone to call me by that nickname."

"Why? Can you honestly say you like your name? Charles Henry Covington?" He sent the pigskin back to his friend, the man who had been by his side since college. "That name is for someone with a stick up their ass. Doesn't fit you, Chuck. Not one bit."

"Same old argument, Lance. You know it's never going to change my mind." Chuck lifted his beer can, and in his poor attempt at a British accent, said, "I actually am quite fond of my name, sir. Charles Henry Covington comes from a long line of bluebloods."

He held his glass of scotch. "More like a line of misfits and horse thieves."

They laughed and took long drinks from their beverages.

Another major bump from the turbulence caused their drinks to spill.

"Damn, what a waste of good scotch." Lance grinned as he wiped up the mess.

"How long has it been since we've been to one of Michael Chamberlain's infamous parties?"

"Almost a year." They'd been fast friends with Michael. Unlike Lance and Chuck, the fellow billionaire had been born with several silver spoons in his mouth.

"Didn't he hit on you first, Lance?" Chuck liked to tease almost as much as he did.

"Of course he did. Look at this body, buddy. Who wouldn't?"

Chuck laughed. "Me, for one."

"You're not gay, but if you were, you wouldn't be able to keep your hands off of me, I'm sure."

"Are you interested in my hands?" Chuck grinned broadly. "Are you coming out of the closet after all these years, Lance?"

"Yeah. Right. In your dreams. If I were gay, you'd be the last person I'd want to go to bed with."

"You couldn't handle what I've got between my legs, buddy."

They loved teasing each other. Always had. It had begun shortly after the first time they'd shared a woman's bed. Now, sharing women was the norm for them, as was ribbing each other.

"You forget. I've seen your junk, and I wasn't impressed."

"I've seen yours, too, Lance O'Little."

"Ten inches of all-American man meat."

Chuck shook his head. "More like nine, maybe nine and a half, for you. I'm ten."

"Shall I get the ruler out again?"

He and Chuck were like brothers in every way. They'd founded and built up their software company right after college. When O'Leary Global had purchased Archer-Covington Technology, they'd become billionaires at the ripe old age of twenty-four. Now, five years later, they were headed into their thirties.

"Any ideas what you want for your birthday, old man?" Lance had been trying to come up with something that would impress Chuck and pull him out of his gloomy mood of late. "You're not giving me much time to get you a present or plan an event. You've only got a month left in your twenties."

"And you turn thirty a month after me, old man. I will let you know when I come up with something I want."

They continued tossing the football in silence for a while.

"You know, Chuck, when you can have anything your heart desires, most things lose their appeal." For the past year or two, boredom had become the norm. Nothing held any luster or surprise. Even the parties, no matter how lavish, were dull and gray. He and Chuck had reached for the stars and had succeeded. But now, with no dreams left to pursue, he felt lost and adrift. He was pretty sure Chuck felt the same. "Sometimes, I miss the old days." *Not just sometimes. All the time.*

"I agree, buddy. Maybe my present from you could be an additional donation to our foundation?"

"That's a great idea, Chuck." He was proud of their work with the homeless and orphans. "I'm thinking a cool million. Maybe we could expand the focus of the Archer-Covington Foundation."

"To what?"

"To help men with tiny dicks get help."

"Fuck you." Chuck laughed. "I'm bigger."

"You wish."

"Do you think Michael is telling the truth about this town of his,

Lance?"

He knew Chuck better than anyone. Like him, there was a void in his friend's life that needed to be filled. By what? Neither of them had a clue. That's why their days and nights were just one long diversion, going from one party to the next. "It's gotta be called Wilde for a reason."

Out of the blue, Michael had sent them an e-mail to join him in his new residence, a tiny town in Northern Nevada. Michael had been part of the jet set, like them, trekking across the globe from one party to the next. Then, he'd fallen off the map.

"He said in his message that we would love the openness of the citizens. I'm not sure what that means, but I'm intrigued."

"So am I, Chuck. So am I."

"Regardless, we always have a great time when we're with Michael."

* * * *

Chuck stepped off the jet and onto the tarmac with Lance following behind.

"That last thirty minutes of our flight was no picnic," Lance said, referring to the turbulence.

"I agree. It's nice to be on old mother earth again."

"Welcome to Nevada, guys." Michael stood in front of them. "What do you think of my new runway?"

Lance put his arm around their friend's shoulder. "This is yours?"

"I built it for the town." Michael had always had a generous heart. "The grand opening is set for next week."

"Pretty short runway," Chuck teased. "Nothing commercial can land here."

"If you want to build something bigger, Chuck, be my guest. Anything you want to do to help develop this area would be great."

"Michael, have you changed? Where is the fun-loving, sun-seeking, Peter Pan, gay guy we partied with on Depp's yacht at Cannes two years ago?"

"Still here. That's why I love this place. I'm sure you will love it, too." Michael led them to his car, a stretch limo. The driver opened the door for them. "Thanks, Neil." They all got inside the stretch. "Actually, I asked you here for a reason. I've got some things I want to talk to both of you about."

"You brought us here to pitch something?" Lance frowned. "Michael, you know we are retired."

"At thirty years old? Lance, you guys have to be tired of playing. Right?"

He and Lance shrugged.

"Guys, isn't it time for something more rewarding? You built an incredible business together. Don't you miss that feeling you had back then?"

Michael had hit the nail on the head, but Chuck wasn't about to let him know it. He wondered what their friend was up to. Why had he brought them here? "What are you selling, Michael?"

"Wilde, Nevada. My town."

Lance's eyebrows shot up. "It sounds like you've put down roots here."

"I have. I think you two will see why once I show you around. It's like no other place in the world, and as you know, I've seen a whole lot of the world. The citizens are the most open-armed, wonderful, nonjudgmental people I've ever seen."

Lance smiled. "So you only want us for our money, not our good looks."

"Guys, I'm serious. I'm funding tons of projects around town. The family who owns the mine is jumping in, too. I've built a resort for gay clientele already. It opens next month. We are also founding a college, plus many more projects that I hope you'll be interested in."

"Oh my God, Michael. Have you lost your way?" Lance held out his hand. "I want your party card right now. You sound like one of those uptight suits Chuck and I dealt with in New York when we first started A&C."

"We all have to grow up sometime, Lance. Even you." Michael smiled. "You are two of my best friends. Your money would be appreciated, but isn't required. I just wanted you to see my town for yourselves." He pointed out the window to a sign by a turnoff. "That's The Masters' Chambers, the local BDSM club."

That shocked him. "Way out here? In rural Nevada?"

"I'm telling you guys, this place is special. For instance, the normal family makeup is not one guy and one girl."

"You mean it's a gay town?" Lance asked.

Michael laughed. "Not exactly, though people in Wilde accept gays completely. Most families consist of multiple partners. One of the most common is two men and one woman."

Lance nodded. "Now you're talking my kind of language."

"I remember you two liked to share," Michael said. "Do you still?"

"We do." Chuck had never dreamed that he and Lance would ever be able to share a woman beyond a night or two. He'd always thought that one day they would have to go their separate ways to wives and lives of their own. Listening to Michael talk about his new town, he wondered if there was a chance of having a different kind of life, one where his best friend in the world could build a family with him.

"Tell us more, Michael." Lance's curiosity was certainly as peaked as his. "Tell us everything."

"I think it's time for you to see for yourselves. I'm sure you're both hungry. Let's start your tour at Norma's, the local diner. They serve up the best pancakes you've ever tasted in your life. They call them King Cakes, for Elvis Presley, who visited Wilde years ago."

Chapter Two

With her mind still on what the sheriff had told her, Danielle started a new pot of coffee. It had felt good to talk to someone about her past after all these years. Sheriff Champion had promised to keep her secret, and she believed he would.

The diner was thinning out like normal this time of day, but the next shift in the silver mine was about to start. No time to rest. They had about thirty minutes until those ending their shift would arrive at the diner to be fed. Anna, the other waitress, had struggled through the rush, clearly under the weather with allergies or a cold. Danielle had suggested she go home, but the stubborn woman refused.

Justin Champion, one of the sheriff's sons, sat in a booth by himself. He was on his third cup of coffee. She had an idea as to why he was here, away from his wife, Shelby.

Danielle walked over with a pitcher of water. "Tell me the truth, Justin. Your dad sent you here to keep an eye out for me, right?"

He shrugged. "What can I tell you? My dad thinks the world of you, Danielle. I'm first shift. Besides, haven't you heard? I'm the new deputy in Wilde."

"I hadn't. When did that happen?"

"We kept it quiet for a while. Dad wanted to make sure I was happy with my decision. When I assured him I was, he swore me in. That was just a couple of days ago."

"What about the rodeo school you and Deuce are running for boys? Will you have time for it still with your new duties?"

"Sure will. When we have a class in town, Dad will give me the week off."

"How long will you be my bodyguard?"

"For as long as necessary. Brandon will take second shift after he gets out of court. Alex has agreed to the third shift."

"How long can you guys keep that up? A few days? A week? Shelby isn't going to want her men away for too long, will she?"

"Shelby knows about the cartel's interest in you. She's glad we can help."

"Who is helping Mackenzie's brother? Does Trent have bodyguards, too?" Danielle hated what Mackenzie's brother had been through. Trent had been Malcolm's prisoner for much longer than she had. She couldn't imagine the torture Trent had endured.

"Yes. The Masters brothers have stepped up for the job of keeping an eye out for their new brother-in-law."

"I'm sure Mackenzie is happy about that."

"She is," Justin said. "We're all going to support him for however long it takes. It's going to be a long road before Trent is back to normal."

"A very long road. I can't get over how this place circles the wagons whenever they think someone is in trouble."

"I know what you mean. I love it here."

Like her, Justin and his brothers hadn't grown up in town. Though Elko, their hometown, was less than fifty miles from Wilde, it was as different as night and day.

She filled his water glass. "I didn't ask for a bodyguard, but it's nice to know someone has my back. Thank you."

"You're welcome."

"Would you like a piece of pie? It'll be my treat."

"That would be great, Danielle."

She left to retrieve his dessert.

Anna, the other waitress, came over. "I'm sorry to have to leave you like this, but honestly I can't stay any longer. I called Carlotta. She'll be in to help you with the next rush. She's driving here now from the ranch she and Deuce just bought."

Carlotta was the owner of Norma's Diner and quite the character. She also owned Carlotta's Liquor Store and Tarot Card Reading Room. An odd combination, but in Wilde, it worked. Carlotta was the local psychic, and many went to her for readings. Danielle had never gone to her, though the dear woman had offered several times. She didn't believe in such things. In fact, she didn't believe in much, only herself.

"I'll finish my side work before I leave," Anna said.

Danielle could tell by how flushed Anna's face was that she had to be burning up with fever. "Go home. I can handle this just fine. Feel better."

"But if I get the napkin dispensers and salt and pepper shakers filled, that will make it easier on you."

She shook her head. "No. Just go. I've got it covered, Anna."

"Okay. I swear when you need a favor, I'll be there for you."

"I know you will."

Anna left.

Danielle wiped off the tables and collected her tips. The people of Wilde were so generous. There wasn't a day that went by that she didn't pocket a lot of money.

The bell on the entrance door chimed.

"Have a seat anywhere. I'll be with you in a second." She looked up from her work and saw Michael with two very handsome men.

Although she wasn't interested in any man, she did appreciate a good-looking guy, and lucky for her, there were two delicious pieces of eye candy right in front of her.

They took a seat at one of the tables, their eyes locking in on hers.

She walked over to them. She knew Michael was wealthy, and by the look of the other two men's clothes and the Rolexes on their wrists, she bet they were, too. She handed all three of them menus. "What would you gentlemen like to drink?"

"You know me better than that, Danielle. I'm no gentleman," Michael teased. "And I can assure you that neither are these two."

The one with the dimpled chin and blue eyes spoke first. "I really don't care what I have to drink if you'll join us."

"Thank you, gentlemen, but I'm working."

"Danielle, be careful with these two. They bite." Michael pointed to the one who had invited her to sit. "This is Lance Archer, and this is Charles Covington."

I'm the one who bites. She held up her ticket pad in one hand and her pen in the other. "Now, what can I get for you?"

Charles had dark eyes and the cutest grin she'd ever seen. "I'll take a glass of iced tea with lots of your sugar in it."

Lance and Charles were barking up the wrong tree.

"Iced tea it is." Without waiting for a response, she turned on her heels and headed to the drink station. She glanced back at their table and her eyes locked in to the hungry stares of Lance and Charles.

She shook her head. *Just because they are rich, I guess they think they can have anything or anyone they want. I'll show them a thing or two.*

Bringing the three glasses of tea back to their table, she looked them straight in the eyes.

"Don't we get our sugar, sweetheart? That's what I ordered." The one named Charles winked.

This is the last straw. Pretending to stumble, she tilted the tray with the glasses, sending them and their contents to the table. The tea splashed, covering Lance and Charles, with a few drops hitting Michael.

"I'm so sorry, gentlemen." She was unable to hide her smile. "Let me get something to clean up this mess."

Michael burst into laughter. "You don't mess with Wilde women, guys. I warned you."

Justin came up behind her. "Everything okay, Danielle?"

She giggled and nodded. "I'm fine."

The looks on the faces of Lance and Charles were priceless. But their shock quickly turned to laughter, too.

Justin turned his attention to the two new arrivals. "And you gentlemen are?"

Michael slapped the table, lost to his hysterics. "The cavalry has arrived." He turned to Lance and Charles. "I also told you how protective the men of Wilde are about the women around here. Now you're in for it." Another round of laughter from Michael sent her into a fit of giggles until tears were rolling down her cheeks.

Justin didn't laugh.

"I guess we got what we deserved." Charles stood and extended his hand to Justin. "I'm Charles Covington, sir. This is my friend and business partner, Lance Archer. We are friends of Michael."

Justin shook hands with him. "I'm Justin Champion. Looks like Danielle has everything under control here. That is, if she can stop laughing."

"I–I–I can't breathe," she said, trying to stifle her giggles.

Lance stood and walked next to her. "I guess we got started on the wrong foot."

"Let me help you clean this up," Charles told her.

"We'll both help her, Chuck."

"Chuck?" She grinned. "That's the name of our cook. Perhaps you can handle the kitchen, too."

"I've got it," Michael said. "You two should talk to Carlotta about getting jobs at the diner. I'm sure you would make excellent waitresses. That way, you could spend time with Danielle. That's probably the only way you'll get to." Once again, he burst into laughter.

"Shut up, Chamberlain. Tell him, Chuck." Lance smiled. "This is ridiculous."

"My name is Charles, not Chuck." The brown-eyed hunk glared at his friend.

"I actually like the name Chuck," she confessed.

"Then I'm Chuck from now on." He grinned. "After we help you clean up the tea, may we stay and order something to eat, miss?"

"I think that will be just fine, but keep in mind, I'm even better with mashed potatoes."

"Oh my God. That would be funny." Michael howled. "I can see it now."

She cracked up, delirious in the hilarity of the moment.

Justin joined in the fun and started to chuckle. The laughter was extremely contagious. She couldn't remember the last time she'd laughed so hard. It felt good.

"Come with me, you two. I'll get you a towel to dry off with."

They followed her as the door to the diner opened with the first miners who would want to eat their lunch.

"Are you the only waitress today?" Chuck asked.

"For a bit. The other girl went home sick, but the owner is headed this way to help me out." She turned to the stream of customers coming in the door. "Sit anywhere you like. I'll be with you in a moment."

"Looks like you could use some help." Lance had a playful charm that drew her in. "Let us hand out the menus and get the drinks set up."

She gave him and Chuck each a dry towel. "That's okay. I've got this."

Chuck scanned the room. "Every table is full." He grabbed her hand gently. "Let us help you out. It's the least we can do. This is how we worked our way through college."

Had they come from meager beginnings, too?

"You waited tables before?"

"Yes." Chuck's smile made her tingle. "And we also were bartenders."

Michael had been born rich. She'd heard about his upbringing from Jessie Wilde, who had known him since they were children. Danielle had incorrectly thought that Lance and Chuck, being his friends, must have come from the same kind of family.

"Just give us the pad and pencils, Danielle." Lance's smile melted her heart. "We've got this under control."

Her first impression had been wrong about him and Chuck. They weren't spoiled trust-fund boys. "You have a deal, but only until Carlotta shows, okay? Then your lunch is on me."

"Perfect."

"Here, put these on." She handed them aprons. "They will cover up the tea stains. I would suggest you put your watches in your pockets for safe keeping."

"Pretty and smart. Quite the combo," Lance said.

She smiled. "Don't start that again."

He held up both his hands in mock surrender. "You win."

"Good. Now, let's get these people fed."

Lance and Chuck went to work. They hadn't been lying about their experience. Norma's was packed, but everyone was being taken care of. They even had the cook laughing. Lance started calling him Little Chuck, which seemed to suit him fine.

Halfway through the rush, Michael walked over to her. "Danielle, I've got to leave and meet with Austin. Looks like Lance and Chuck are enjoying themselves."

It did to her, too.

"When you get finished, please tell them my driver will be waiting to take them to my place."

Finished with them? She had sworn off men long ago.

"Sure thing, Michael. I'll let them know where it is."

For years, she'd been moving from place to place. Not the best situation, but one she had lived with in order to remain hidden from her family. Having to leave a place at a moment's notice didn't allow her to have attachments.

Danielle was so impressed by Lance and Chuck. They worked like fiends. But it didn't matter. Once this shift was over, she would send them on their way. That would be the end of it. Had to be.

Carlotta ran in, arriving at the end of the rush. "Danielle, I'm so...Oh my God. How in da vorld did you handle da lunch run by yourself?" In her mid-sixties, the woman had more fire than most. Today, she wore a long red skirt and a white top. Her black, wavy hair, obviously dyed, hung to her shoulders. She was a character, through and through. Carlotta had been so good to Danielle, giving her a job the first day of her arrival in town. "And how did you get every table cleaned? I've never seen da diner looking so nice. Did da customers no show?"

Danielle loved her Eastern European accent, though everyone in town had learned it was only an act. She actually spoke quite well whenever the love of her life was around, cowboy champion Deuce.

"I didn't." Carlotta was like a mother to Danielle, unlike her own biological mother had been. "I had help. Those two over there walked in, saw I was overwhelmed, and took up the slack."

Lance and Chuck were sweeping and mopping the place.

"Dey did? Dey're not from here." Carlotta studied them for a moment, her eyes softening. "I'm so sorry, Danielle. I vas late. I had a flat tire. I had to call Deuce to help me."

"That's okay. As you can see, we handled it."

"You and dese two fine-looking men did a vonderful job." Carlotta looked at her with knowing eyes. Clearly, the woman could see the attraction she had for them. *Maybe she is really psychic.* "Danielle, how much did ve make?"

"I was about to run the hourly report," she told her. "Let's see." When the figure showed up on the cash register's screen, her jaw dropped. It was nearly twice the normal take.

"Dat is amazing. Da dree of you handled dat kind of volume by yourselves?"

"Us and the cook, Little Chuck." Lance walked over to them. "You must be Carlotta."

"Da vone and only," her boss told him. "Carlotta Angelina Bianca Sollomovici."

"That's Big Chuck, ma'am, the one with the mop in his hand. His real name is Charles Covington. I'm Lance Archer."

"I see. Dank you. I'm sure you two must be hungry."

"Starving," he said as Chuck walked up next to him.

"Den I must remedy dat. How vould you like a big juicy steak? It's da least I can do for da help you gave sveet Danielle."

"I would love that."

"Excellent," Carlotta headed to the swinging door to the kitchen. "Have a seat. How do you like your steaks?"

Lance smiled broadly. "Medium, for me."

"Well done, thank you." Chuck sat down in a booth.

"Very good. I vill bring you some applications to fill out. I could use two strong men like you at my diner."

Chuck shrugged. "But ma'am—"

"No buts about it, young man. You've proved your vorth to me. I've made up my mind about dis."

Lance slid into the booth, sitting across from Chuck.

"And I vant to give you both a free reading. I'm a psychic, you know."

They both shook their heads. Carlotta had them under her spell, which made her giggle again.

"No arguing, understand?" She didn't wait for a response as she headed into the kitchen.

"That was fun," Chuck said.

"I agree, buddy. We haven't had this much fun in years. Didn't you just love the people?"

"They're amazing." Lance placed a wad of bills on the table. "You and I worked at five-star restaurants and never made this kind of money."

Chuck brought out his tips, adding them to Lance's. "I know. There's got to be at least nine hundred dollars there."

Danielle was shocked to see the pile. "Wilde folks are very generous. I've always made good tips, but nothing like this."

"I told you, Danielle," Lance said. "We're experienced waiters. Service with a smile."

He and Chuck pushed the money toward her. "This is for you."

"I couldn't. You earned that fair and square."

"Will you at least go out with us?" Chuck asked.

Lance chimed in, "On a real date?"

God, she wanted to say yes. They were kind, wonderful men. Handsome and charming. What woman wouldn't want to go out with them? But she couldn't.

"I'm sorry, guys." She had to remain detached. *I've stayed too long in Wilde.* Was telling the sheriff about her past a mistake? She wasn't sure. This town had become home to her, and she didn't want to leave. Not yet. Sure it would be amazing to spend time with Lance and Chuck, but she couldn't. It wouldn't be fair to them. "I just can't say yes." She headed into the kitchen, leaving them behind.

Chapter Three

"What just happened?" Lance stared at the swinging door that Danielle had just left through. She'd turned their offer down, and that didn't sit well with him. Not one damn bit.

"I haven't got a clue." Chuck shook his head. "Maybe she could see through our BS. She's clearly the kind of woman who doesn't take crap from anyone." He lifted his apron and pointed to the tea stain on his shirt. "Case in point."

"I'm not ready to give up, buddy." Just because he and Chuck had lost the battle didn't mean they had to lose the war. "I want a date with this girl. Let's go with the old tried and true, send-the-flower bit."

"Good idea. I wonder if this town has a florist."

"We'll have to ask Michael."

Chuck looked around. "Where is he, anyway?"

"He left about halfway through the rush." Norma's Diner had been so much more fun than all the posh parties he and Chuck had attended in the last several years. "That was a blast, wasn't it?"

"More fun than I've had in a very long time, and I know that gorgeous brunette had a lot to do with it."

He agreed wholeheartedly. "Danielle made it fun. She is so sassy and beautiful. Just our type."

"You can say that again."

"She's the whole package." Being billionaire bachelors, he and Chuck were used to women throwing themselves at them. But not Danielle. She was worth the chase, and God, he liked the chase. "Long, dark hair. Green eyes. Curves to die for. And so very sweet. I would give anything to hear her laugh again."

"Me, too. It's contagious."

Carlotta came in carrying a tray with their meal. The aroma and sizzle of the steaks made his stomach growl. He was hungry. She sat the plates in front of them.

"Here are some hot rolls for you, gentlemen. Save room for dessert."

Lance looked back at the swinging door. "Is Danielle okay?"

The woman's gaze landed on him. "Your aura is quite impressive, young man. You have a caring heart. I can see dat. Yes, she is fine, but I dink she needs time alone for now. I have a message for you." She handed him a piece of paper. "I hope it is good news."

Obviously, Danielle hadn't shared its contents with her.

He opened it up, expecting the worst. Thankfully, it wasn't. Danielle wasn't blowing them off completely. It was only a message from Michael, stating his driver would be just outside to take them back to his place once they were ready to leave the diner.

He handed the note to Chuck. "Everything is fine."

"Dat's good to hear," Carlotta said.

Chuck read the message. "Yes, it is."

"Now, about your new jobs. Be here at ten tomorrow morning. All I'm going to have you do is fill out some paperwork." She handed him an envelope filled with cash. "Dis is your tip money. No argument. Danielle told me you vould try to refuse, but you earned it. You both look tired, so sleep in. Dat's it. Understand?"

He smiled. "Carlotta, we—"

Chuck held up his hand. "Wait a second, Lance. I think this is a great opportunity for us."

Carlotta nodded. "Lance, your friend Charles is someone you should listen to."

"Please call me Chuck, ma'am."

That shocked him.

"Excellent. I'll see you both at ten. I vill bring my cards. I vant to read you both. Enjoy your meal." Carlotta went back into the kitchen where Danielle was.

Lance silently cursed the swinging door that separated him from the gorgeous woman who had spilled tea on his shirt. "What was that all about? You want us to take jobs here at Norma's. We're billionaires, Chuck."

"Carlotta doesn't know that. Besides, I think Danielle won't be able to avoid us if we end up working with her at the diner."

There was the Chuck he knew in college. "Ah. You're a devious bastard, aren't you?"

"Takes one to know one, Lance."

* * * *

Danielle heard the bell on the entrance door jingle. She peeked through the food window to the dining room and saw Lance and Chuck leaving. She felt her shoulders relax.

"Are dey gone?" Carlotta asked.

"They are, thank God. Now I can get some work done before the diner crowd arrives."

"Not just yet, young lady. Dere's something ve're going to do."

"What's that?"

"Come vith me," Carlotta headed to the back door. "Lil' Chuck, you keep an eye on da place for me."

"Is that going to be my name from now on? Lil' Chuck?" the cook asked, smiling. "I kinda like it. I also like Lance and Big Chuck."

"So do I," Carlotta said. "Come on, Danielle."

There was no sense in arguing with her boss. Once she made up her mind about something, there was no stopping her until it was done.

They got in her car. "Where are you taking me?"

Carlotta smiled. "I've been vanting to read you for a very long time. No time like da present."

"Alright. Lead the way, Madam." Danielle cared for the self-proclaimed psychic.

Carlotta had the most giving heart she'd ever known. Danielle had been avoiding sitting down in front of the sweet woman and getting her fortune told since arriving in Wilde. Although she didn't believe in it, she was still afraid Carlotta might find out something about her past. *Maybe if I hold my breath or think about kittens, she won't be able to get inside my head with her mumbo jumbo.*

Maybe I believe a little. Danielle grinned.

Carlotta's other business was just outside of town on the highway. Her boss parked the car. They walked into Carlotta's Liquor Store and Tarot Card Reading Room. Danielle had never been inside the space.

As they went in, the first thing she heard was trancelike music, which made her smile. *So like Carlotta.* Four statues of Buddha were in the corners of the room. She could smell sweet incense burning. Other than that, it looked like most package stores she'd seen. Several shelves of liquor and wine lined the walls. In the center were racks of wine from all over the world. The art on the wall did remind her of what gypsies might have in their wagons.

"Hey, boss." The young man behind the counter seemed surprised to see Carlotta. "I didn't expect you so early."

"I have a reading, Owen."

"Danielle, you're finally giving in. Good for you. You won't be disappointed. Carlotta has real talent."

"You know da drill. Do not disturb us until ve are done."

"Yes, ma'am."

Danielle felt a shiver go up and down her spine. The sheriff already knew her secret. She didn't want anyone else to find out about her past, not even Carlotta.

The fortune-teller led her past Owen and to the opening that had beads blocking the view beyond.

The room they walked into was draped in fabrics of every color. In the center was a small table covered in a blue tablecloth. On its surface was a crystal ball. Three chairs were around the table, two metal ones and a large black leather wingback that was clearly meant for Carlotta.

"Sit, child." Carlotta reached under the table. She pulled out a white turban which had a large crystal stone centered on it and a deck of tarot cards. "Ve von't be needing dis today." She removed the crystal ball. "It vouldn't vork vell since you are an unbeliever."

"I never said that."

"So you do believe?"

She grinned. "I believe in you, Carlotta. Always will."

The sweet lady smiled, making her look even prettier. "And I believe in you, Danielle. More dan you do in yourself. I believe you can have happiness in dis life."

She wished she could believe that, too. "How does this work?"

"Let's see vhat da spirits tell us." Carlotta shuffled the cards several times. She patted the deck and created three piles on the table. "Don't touch. Just point to da vone dat you are most drawn to, my dear."

"I like them all."

Carlotta shook her finger. "Don't try to stall, Danielle. This von't hurt. I promise."

She wasn't so sure. *Please don't let her see into my past.* "This one." She pointed at the middle pile.

Carlotta picked up the pile, moving the others to the side. "I shall use the five-card spread for you. Da first is your distant past. Da second is your near past. Da one in da middle is the present. Da fourth is your near future. Da final card is your distant future. Simple as dat." She turned over five cards in a row on the table.

Danielle looked at the first card, which was of a stately woman wearing a crown of twelve stars. "You said this one is of my distant past, right?" She held her breath.

"Dat is correct." Carlotta bent over the cards. "This is da Empress in the reversed position." The fortune-teller's eyes lifted from the table and locked in on her. "You had a very tragic childhood. Your mother vasn't kind to you, vas she?"

Oh, God. Please don't let her see anything more. "Doesn't everyone have dysfunction in their families?"

"I suppose so, but yours vas filled with selfishness, pain, jealousy, and rage. Your father died when you were very young."

"I miss my real father," she confessed, starting to really believe in Carlotta's gift. "I was only five when he died."

"Your mother vas blinded and confused."

That's putting it mildly.

Carlotta grabbed her hand. "Da card tells me dat she's not been in your life in a very long time."

Danielle's heart was pounding hard in her chest. "I should get back to the diner, Carlotta."

"Not before ve finish your reading, child." Carlotta released her hand. "Dis is da Five of Staffs, my dear, though some call them vands. It is in da position of your near past. You've been struggling, hoping to reach some destination, but never arriving. You've been in Vilde for two years now, yes?"

"Yes," she whispered, in awe of how clearly Carlotta was seeing into her past.

"How long at da last place before dis one?"

She didn't answer, couldn't answer.

"Ah. A short time. And I can see dat da places you resided in are only stopping points. Vilde has been da longest you've stayed anywhere since running avay from your family."

"I'm sorry, Carlotta. I don't want to do this any more."

"Child, I'm like a priest. Anyding da cards show me is sacred. I vill not talk. You understand? You are safe vith me."

That made her feel a little better.

"Shall I continue? Vould you like to see vhat da present is like…and your future?"

She nodded. Her life had been nothing but running for so very long. Carlotta had proven that she was real, that her cards were real. Could the days ahead be different? Could her demons from the past be dead?

"Dis is da Six of Swords. You have left an untenable situation and are charting a new course. Da passage from darkness to light can be difficult. You belong in Vilde. You must trust in yourself, Danielle."

"The road has already been long and hard."

Her friend sighed. "Yes. I sense dat it has."

Very long and very hard.

"Dis is the near future. Da Lovers." Carlotta closed her eyes. "Love is a mystery. Full of its own challenges."

"It's not for me. I don't have time for love."

The sweet fortune-teller's eyes opened and she smiled. "Da spirits dink differently. Your aura changed whenever Lance and Chuck vere near you." She tapped the Lover's card. "Dhey are da reason dis card is here."

"I'm not going out with them. That's final."

"Don't judge dhem so harshly, child. It's clear dhey lack much, but dheir hearts are pure."

"Speaking of hearts…" Danielle wanted to get the conversation off of the two men she couldn't stop thinking about. "This card in my far future looks scary. A heart with three swords piercing it. When will it happen?"

"Da distant future can mean next week or next year or ten years from now, but I sense what da Three of Swords is signifying is closer dan you dink."

"What does it mean?" A cold chill overtook her and she began to tremble.

"Da past you've been running from, Danielle, is about to catch up vith you."

Shocked by Carlotta's reading, she stood. "Oh my God."

The woman grabbed her hands and squeezed. "You are not alone in Vilde, my dear. I vill support you, and dhere are many others ready to do da same. You are one of us now. You vill be safe vith us. Da spirits say so."

She wanted to believe that. With all her heart, she wanted to. But she'd been alone for so long that she just couldn't.

"Don't forget." Carlotta held up the Lover's card. "Lance and Chuck are here for a reason. Dhey are here for you. Perhaps da universe brought dhem here not only to heal your heart, but to protect you also."

"Thank you, Carlotta. I really hope you're right."

"The cards never lie, Danielle. You'll see."

Chapter Four

No matter how hard she tried, Danielle couldn't seem to fall asleep. Her mind was racing like mad. Carlotta's reading had unnerved her, and she couldn't get the images of Lance and Chuck out of her head.

She needed to sleep since she had to report to the diner in the morning for her shift.

Turning on the television to a documentary about elephants, she hoped it would lull her just enough to forget the two rich bad boys, allowing her some shut-eye.

The announcer's delivery was soft and soothing. The background music was melodic and pleasing.

"The elephant is the largest mammal living outside the oceans. In Africa, their herds' ranges extend over many countries and thousands of miles."

She sipped her wine as a mother elephant and her baby appeared on the screen. They looked so cute together. She'd never had time for relationships, being on the run for so long.

Still a virgin. Twenty-two years old. Crazy.

The picket fence and loving children were always out of reach. A normal life would never be hers.

She sat her empty glass on her nightstand and leaned back on her pillows.

"Their trunks are very versatile and are used for communication, as seen by this mother with her calf. Like a human's hand, the elephant's trunk can handle objects…"

She yawned. The magic of the documentary was working.

"…when the female comes into heat, the males will find her…"

* * * *

Danielle looked at the African sun, which was low on the horizon and the most beautiful orange she'd ever seen. She walked by a crystal blue stream. The sky was clear and dotted by white puffy clouds. The air was warm. She wore no clothes and no shoes, which allowed her skin to feel the heat of the setting sun and her toes to be tickled by the softness of the grass.

The birds sang beautifully. This was a perfect day.

She came across a blanket that was stretched out with a picnic of all her favorite foods and wine. Kneeling down, she wondered where the owners of this outdoor feast might be. Would they miss a few bites of fruit and a sip of wine? Feeling hungry and a little naughty, she decided to go for it. There wasn't a soul around for miles.

Off in the distance, elephants were drinking from the stream. The baby calves were so cute.

She grabbed one of the strawberries and took a bite. It was the juiciest, sweetest fruit she'd ever tasted in her life. She ate another one. And another one. Then she ate some of the cheese, which was just as delicious as the strawberries had been. The wine was open, sitting in an ice bucket. She poured the golden liquid into a glass. She brought the rim of the goblet to her lips and tasted the sweet wine.

Laughing, she looked up into the sky. Then she heard footsteps coming her direction. Guilt for what she'd done swamped her. She wanted to run, to hide. But suddenly, she couldn't move. It would be better to explain to the picnickers she'd stolen from how hungry she'd been and that she would gladly pay them back for what she'd taken. Reasonable people would understand, and she prayed they would be of that mind, too.

Looking up, she saw two men headed her way. They both wore aprons that were stained by tea. Something in her mind tried to bring up a memory. Had she poured tea on these two men? What were their names? Lance and Chuck. She remembered them.

As they got closer, she saw that they wore only the aprons and nothing else. Very strange. Then she looked down at her own body, and recalled that she was naked, too. Her face got so very hot. She tried to tug on the corner of the blanket to cover herself, but it wouldn't budge. There was no place to hide. There was no place to run.

"What do we have here, Chuck?" Lance asked, grinning.

His eyes wandered over her body, taking her in. "A common thief is what I see."

"Please forgive me." She was trembling. "I was hungry. I only ate a few strawberries and had a couple of sips of wine."

"What shall we do with you?" Lance's husky tone made her tingle. "This is Africa. Stealing is not tolerated."

"She must be punished." Chuck's gaze burned into her hotter than the sun. "You and I both know that. She knows it, too."

"I promise to pay you back. Please. I'm so sorry."

Lance bent down and grabbed her by the hair. "You're a pretty thing, aren't you? Too bad you stole from us. I think we must spank her, Chuck. Do you agree?"

"I do. Let's tie her to that tree."

She looked the direction Chuck was pointing. How had she not noticed that tree before?

The sexy men removed their aprons. She gazed at their muscled frames. They were the most beautiful men she'd ever seen. Lance swept her up in his arms and carried her to the tree. They tugged on their aprons until they were long ropes which they used to tie her to the tree.

They freely touched her body with their hands.

Lance cupped her ass. "Time for your punishment, thief."

Chuck fondled her breasts. "Time to pay for your crimes."

They slapped her ass again and again, and although it stung, she felt sensations in her body she'd never experienced before. Heat rolled through her with every smack. Tears welled in her eyes and she chewed on her lower lip.

"I believe this little beauty has learned her lesson." Lance grinned wickedly. "It's time to show her that we forgive her for her evil deeds."

Chuck kissed her cheek. "Let's untie her and place her on the blanket so we can get a better look at her gorgeous body."

As they laid her on the blanket, she wanted them to look, but she didn't understand exactly why.

Lance touched her breasts. "These are so beautiful. God, you are a knockout, Danielle."

He remembers my name. The more he caressed her, the more her desires increased.

"She's perfect." Chuck put his lips on her belly and began to kiss her, moving his mouth lower and lower.

Her head was spinning. Why was her body reacting like this? It was as if it had a mind of its own. A sea of sensations washed over her that she couldn't quite understand, but she loved the feelings their touches of forgiveness were inciting in her.

Moisture pooled between her thighs. A dizzy heat spread through her, and her need for more grew and grew. *More of what?* She didn't know. So much pressure was building inside her that she thought she might actually explode.

Lance kissed her. "What's a virgin doing in the middle of the savanna?"

He knows I've never made love. "Please don't stop. Please."

"We won't." His confidence was intoxicating.

Chuck leaned forward, the heat from his body overwhelming her. "We want to show you how much you mean to us."

"But we only just met," she panted.

She could feel his hot breath on her pussy. "Doesn't matter, sweetheart. We will never let you go. You ate our food and drank our wine. You are ours now. That's the law."

"I am yours." She felt her heart surrendering to them.

Their hands and lips skated over her body, raising her desires even more than before. She fisted the blanket. "Please. I've never felt this before. Please. Take me."

"We will. All of you," Lance said.

The elephants trumpeted in the background, and the announcer's voice was heard. "This program was brought to you by the O'Leary Global Foundation and by the donations of generous people like you."

"What's that?" Chuck's confusion was evident on his face.

Lance's body began to fade. "Who is that?"

"It's just the television," she told them. "Please, don't stop."

"A television in Africa?" Chuck asked before vanishing.

She reached for Lance, but he, too, disappeared.

"No." She opened her eyes, wishing the dream hadn't ended.

Her pussy was soaked, but she was back in her bed in Nevada. Her body continued to buzz.

Unlike in the dream, Danielle knew what she needed. But the two sexy beasts weren't here.

She opened her nightstand drawer and settled for second best. Mr. Wonderful.

Hopefully her vibrator would take her back to Africa and back to Lance and Chuck.

* * * *

Chuck rolled out of bed. He looked at the clock on the wall. It was 8:10 in the morning. He hadn't gotten up this early in years. Too many parties. Ever since he and Lance had sold the business, their lives had been one long never-ending party. But yesterday at the diner with Danielle had been the most fun he'd had in years. He'd dreamed about her. God, he hadn't been able to get her out of his head ever since she'd spilled the tea on him and Lance.

A knock at the door pulled him from his thoughts. "Come in."

The door opened and Lance walked in. "I forgot that there was an eight o'clock in the morning. How about you?"

Chuck yawned. "Same here, but I'm wide awake now."

"You better get up and get ready, buddy." Lance smiled. "We have an appointment with our new boss at ten this morning, remember?"

"Of course I remember." They'd get to see Danielle again, work with her. Make her want them. "Where's Michael? Still in bed?"

"Nope. Apparently this place got to him, too," Lance replied. "He woke me up ten minutes ago."

Party boy Michael was up before them? "That's not the Michael I remember. He was always the last to rise."

Lance nodded in agreement. "But he's changed. You're not going to believe this, but he's been up since six. Told me he was going to get us some breakfast and a newspaper. He should be back in fifteen minutes."

"That's enough time for me to shower and get dressed." Chuck pushed back the heavy blanket covering him and stood up.

"Me, too." Lance turned to leave but stopped before he got out the door. He faced Chuck again. "He's got quite the place here, doesn't he?"

"Yes, he does." Michael had lived all around the world in some of the most lavish places imaginable. His new home wasn't like any of the others. "It's simple. Michael Chamberlain living in a log cabin. The old crowd would be stunned."

"It's not your typical log cabin, Chuck. Has to be at least five thousand square feet."

"True." Chuck laughed. "It's not rustic by any means. Those leather sofas in the main room look Italian to me. They must've cost a fortune."

"And did you get a load of the pool and hot tub?"

"Amazing. Michael does need his creature comforts." He always had, even in college. "Still, it's made of logs. Michael has been breathing this Northern Nevada air for over a year now. He is different."

"He looks happy." Lance stared out the large window in Chuck's room. He had a wonderful view of the mountains. "Maybe we should consider staying longer. The air might do us good, Chuck."

And the girl who had invaded my dreams. "We better get going."

"You're right. Michael said to meet us on the back deck where breakfast would be served. I'll see you in fifteen minutes." Lance turned and left for his room.

Chuck walked into his bathroom suite.

After getting cleaned up and dressed, he went out the back. The sky was a bright blue. Lance was already sipping coffee. Another guy, wearing a white robe, sat with him.

"Hey, Chuck," The man stood and extended his hand. "I'm Harry Morgan, Michael's boyfriend."

He shook his hand. "Nice to meet you. Michael told us that he'd found someone special. I'm happy for both of you."

Harry smiled. "Grab yourself a cup of coffee. Michael should be back with food any moment."

As if on cue, the man in question walked in carrying their breakfast. "You two are famous around these parts," he said, laughing.

"What are you talking about?" Lance asked.

Michael bent down and kissed Harry. "We're hosting celebrities, honey. Wilde is all abuzz." Michael laughed and handed the newspaper to his boyfriend.

Harry read a few lines and burst into laughter.

"What in the hell is in there?" Chuck asked. "Are you two pulling our legs?"

Shaking his head, Michael continued laughing uncontrollably, and so did Harry. "Ever since you two showed up, I've laughed more than I have in years. See for yourself. The ladies are organizing a bake sale for you."

"A bake sale?" He took the paper and read the article. The headline sent him over the edge.

"What?" Lance demanded. "Read it."

"Two Homeless Men Wait Tables At Norma's Diner for Food." He died laughing and continued reading through the tears. "Local businesswoman Carlotta Sollomovici, owner of the diner, told several citizens she was impressed by the two men and wanted to lend them a helping hand. The Ladies Auxiliary of Wilde has organized a bake sale that will be held this Saturday to benefit the two new arrivals to town. Maude Strong, president of the club, said this event is exactly what they'd been looking for since their mission has been to stamp out homelessness in Nevada. 'These two unfortunate souls need our help,' she said. 'We hope you will open your hearts and wallets at the bake sale.'"

"Oh my God, these are the sweetest people I've ever known," Lance said through his own chuckles. "We've got to clear this up."

"That explains the big tips we were getting." Chuck realized just how unique Wilde was. "It almost makes me want to be poor."

That sent them all into another crazy fit.

Michael finally composed himself, taking a seat and pouring a cup of coffee. "You see why I brought you here. Wilders care. They have the biggest hearts in the world."

Harry grabbed his hand. "I'm glad you came and settled down here, honey."

"Me, too." Michael turned to them. "Sorry to drop this on you but I have to leave this morning."

"I thought you had business you wanted to discuss with us," Lance said.

"I do, but this is an emergency. I'll be back first thing Monday morning. I'm taking Harry with me. We haven't had much time alone together."

"No we haven't." Harry grabbed Michael's hand. "What's going on?"

"The caretaker at the house on Lake Tahoe called. Raccoons got inside. Apparently one died in the wall. They tore up some of the furniture, too. We've got to check it out. I thought we could make a weekend out of it."

"That sounds wonderful, honey."

Chuck looked at the former Peter Pan of the jet set. He'd found happiness in this rural part of Nevada. Michael was happy. Really happy. Could he be, too? "Oh my God. The flowers we ordered are supposed to be delivered this morning."

"Flowers?" Harry asked.

"It's something me and Chuck do when we're pursuing a beautiful woman." Lance jumped to his feet. "We've got to get to the diner before they arrive. We need to clear this up with Carlotta."

He stood. "I agree. She's such a sweet woman. Let's go."

"Why do you have to rush?" Michael asked. "One bouquet of flowers won't shock anyone, even from two homeless guys like you."

"We didn't send just one."

"Lance and Chuck have done it again. I remember your motto. 'Why do when you can overdo.'" Michael doubled over, lost to another round of laughter. He tossed them some keys. "This is to my Aston Martin. Take it. Harry and I will join you shortly, after we pack. I don't want to miss this. We can hit the road for Tahoe after."

They ran out the door and headed back to Norma's, to Carlotta, and to Danielle, the woman who had come to him in his dreams.

Chapter Five

Danielle swung her legs off the bed as she heard her automatic coffee maker kick on. *God, that was some dream.*

Carlotta had called and told her she didn't have to be at the diner until afternoon. Carlotta and Anna, who was feeling much better, were going to manage the lunch run on their own to make up for leaving her on her own the day before.

She grabbed her robe and walked into the kitchen. The smell of fresh coffee filled the air. She grabbed her mug, filling it with the delicious brew. She inhaled the aroma before taking a sip. She hadn't had a morning of leisure in a long time. *I'm looking forward to it.*

Grabbing a second cup from the cabinet, she filled it to the brim with the steaming liquid and walked to the door. Everyone in Wilde took the newspaper, and she was no exception. The town's mystique reminded her of an earlier era when homes had a single black-and-white TV set and families sat down and ate together.

She opened her door and spotted Dr. Alex Champion in his car parked on the street. She bent down and grabbed up the paper. Alex waved and she headed to him.

He stepped out of his car, scanning every direction.

"I brought you a cup of coffee, Alex. I figured you might like it since you worked the overnight bodyguard shift."

"Thank you. That sounds so good." He took the cup. "This reminds me of my residency. I lived on coffee the whole time."

"I didn't bring any sugar or cream. Do you need any?"

"Black is perfect." He took a sip. "How did you sleep?"

"Like a log," she lied. "I really think your dad is going overboard, don't you?"

"He's sheriff, Danielle. He takes his job very seriously. The cartel isn't something to take lightly."

"You're right, but I do have a gun. I know how to protect myself."

"I'm sure you do." Alex shook his head. "Until my dad gives the green light, you will have bodyguards. My brothers and I will be keeping watch on you. Brandon will be here shortly to take my place."

"I really do appreciate what you, Justin, and Brandon are doing, but I worry about you guys getting enough rest. Shelby is so sweet, allowing you three to do this, but I hate that I'm taking you away from each other."

"Danielle, this will get cleared up before you know it. Dad and Austin are working hard to make sure it does."

"What if it doesn't, Alex? How long will you and your brothers be able to keep this up? Have you thought about that possibility?"

He shrugged. "We'll cross that bridge if we come to it. If, and that's a very big *if*, this lingers for a while, I'm sure we can get some relief bodyguards to fill in from time to time. There's plenty of local single men around town ready to lend a hand to a damsel in distress like yourself."

Her mind instantly brought up images of Lance and Chuck. "Like you said, I guess we'll cross that bridge later."

He gulped down the rest of the coffee and handed her back the cup. "Thank you again."

"No. Thank you. Would you like another cup?"

"No thanks." His cell buzzed. "It's Shelby."

"Please, tell her I said hello and thanks."

"I will." He got back in his car, and she saw his face light up as he began talking to the love of his life.

Danielle walked back into her house. She was renting it from Maude Strong, who was only charging her half what the place should be going for. It was a sweet place—a two-bedroom, one-bath bungalow. *Just perfect for me.*

As always, she patted the book Pauline had given her long ago, her favorite. *Alice's Adventures in Wonderland.* The woman had always been so good to her. She was like a grandmother.

Danielle sat down at her kitchen table, listening to the drips of the leaky faucet, which Maude promised to replace. Actually, the sweet lady was slowly remodeling the whole thing for her. The bathroom fixtures were top of the line, and the appliances were stainless steel. She knew the rent Maude charged her was too little. She smiled, remembering the cookies her landlady had brought her the last time she'd come over to fix an outlet that wasn't working. Maude was a do-it-yourself kind of woman, and she was quite skilled, too. All the women in this town were capable.

Danielle had stayed in Wilde longer than any other place since she turned thirteen years old. Was it too long? The town wasn't on any major highway. It was nestled in the mountains. The best hiding place she'd ever found. *Can I stay?* The sheriff knew about her past now. The last time any of her family had come close to finding her had been five years ago in Kansas City. Maybe they'd finally given up the search.

Was she being foolish to consider staying? Maybe, but she couldn't help it. Once the cartel issue was cleared up, and she prayed Alex was right that it would soon, everything would go back to normal.

She opened the paper, imagining how wonderful it would be to finally call a place home. Even the name of the local newspaper brought a smile to her face. Wonders of Wilde, or as most called it, WOW. She glanced at the headline and her jaw dropped.

"Two Homeless Men Wait Tables At Norma's Diner for Food."

As she continued to read, she thought about the Rolexes Lance and Chuck had put in their pockets yesterday when they'd helped wait tables at the diner. "A bake sale? Oh my God."

She grabbed her cell to call Carlotta. This needed to be cleared up quickly. No answer. She jumped to her feet and headed to the bathroom to get ready.

So much for my leisurely morning.

She had to get to the diner and set the record straight. Lance and Chuck weren't homeless.

I know they are rich.

* * * *

Lance rushed into the diner with Chuck right behind.

"You're early. Very good." Carlotta wore a white turban on her head and a red silk scarf around her neck. She sat at a table with a crystal ball in front of her.

"We need to talk."

"Yes, vee do, but not yet." She pointed to the dozen vases of roses on the counter and shook her finger. "Sit and be quiet."

Lance hoped to explain the mix-up about his and Chuck's financial situation. "But—"

"Quiet. Da spirits are here, and I don't vant dhem to be disturbed. I vill read you now. Sit." She closed her eyes and ran her hands around the crystal ball, never quite touching it.

As she began to hum, he and Chuck sat down. They looked at each other and shrugged. The explanations would have to wait.

"Your hearts are so big, young men. I know you like sveet Danielle, but to use all your tip money for dhese roses vas so foolish."

Lance realized Carlotta believed that was how two supposed homeless men had purchased the flowers. "About that—"

"No talking, please. The vibrations are very sensitive at the moment." The sweet woman opened her eyes and stared into the crystal ball. "Ah. Da spirits tell me dhat you belong vith her." Her gaze lifted to them. "A single rose vould've sufficed."

Lance knew it was way past time to let her know about his and Chuck's fortune, but before he could, Carlotta's attention returned to the ball. Her eyes widened. "This is very odd."

Lance was completely intrigued. "What? What do you see?"

"I see you and Chuck sitting on piles of gold." She smiled, covering the crystal with her silk scarf. "Boys, you might consider buying a lottery ticket. Dis must be your lucky day."

Danielle rushed in, looking so beautiful. Her face was flushed. Behind her came a man.

"Brandon, take a seat over dhere. I need to talk privately vith Danielle and dhese men."

He nodded, sliding into one of the booths.

Lance wondered who the guy was and why he was with Danielle. He spotted a wedding ring on Brandon's finger, putting him at ease.

Before he or Chuck could speak, Danielle started talking so rapidly, her words were running together. "Carlotta, this is my fault. They aren't but Michael is friends and they are, too."

"Slow down, child." Carlotta grinned. "Take a breath."

"I spilled tea on them and they started to help me."

The more she rambled, the more he wanted to sweep her up in his arms and kiss her.

"Another breath, young lady."

"And they don't need this job. Not one bit. Don't you see, Carlotta?"

They all laughed.

Carlotta took off her turban. "I don't understand a dhing, Danielle, you've said. Da spirits speak more clearly dhan you do, my dear."

"Let me explain." Lance told Carlotta how the mix-up happened.

"So you agreed to come vork for me so you could be close to Danielle? Is dhat da real reason?"

Danielle smiled, which pleased him very much.

"We didn't lie, Carlotta." Chuck was trying to worm his way out of this mess. "Plus, you're a tough negotiator. You'd made up your mind we were going to work for you, and it was hard to tell you no. I would love to have you on my side of the table the next time I buy a company."

"Maude vill be so disappointed to cancel da bake sale. It vould be silly to have it for two rich fellows like yourself."

"Don't cancel it, Carlotta." Lance thought the good intentions of the ladies should be rewarded. "Surely there's another charity the money could go to. Chuck and I will double whatever the ladies auxiliary collects."

"That's a great idea, buddy." Chuck turned to Carlotta. "We will also write another check for our own foundation, which benefits orphans and the homeless, in the name of the citizens of Wilde. It's the least we can do for all the confusion we've caused."

"Excellent idea, young man. I'll see to it dhat a retraction is in tomorrow's paper. Too bad. I could've used a couple of good workers like yourselves at my diner."

Danielle giggled. "Anna and I have it covered. I don't want to split tips with these two rich guys. You understand."

"I see how you look at them, child. You're not telling the truth." Carlotta laughed. "The spirits saw it all. Look what these gentlemen sent you."

Danielle turned and looked at the roses on the counter. "How did I miss them?"

"You vere in a rush, that's how." Carlotta stood and grabbed up her crystal ball. "Brandon, come forward. I'm ready to talk vith you."

"Yes, ma'am."

"Da spirits have told me dhat Lance and Chuck are to take over you and your brothers' duties as Danielle's bodyguards."

Lance didn't like the sound of that one bit. "Bodyguards? Why does she need bodyguards?"

Brandon studied him and Chuck for a moment. "You're the homeless guys, right?"

"Actually they're billionaires." Michael walked in through the front door with Harry. "What did I miss?"

"Carlotta says these two are going to take over the bodyguard duty for Danielle," Brandon said. "You know them?"

"Yes, and you can trust them. Brandon Champion, this is Lance Archer and Charles Covington."

"He goes by Chuck now, Michael. Da spirits are telling me that Danielle, Lance, and Chuck need a moment alone." She looked at Brandon, Michael, and Harry. "Gentlemen, come vith me. I have a freshly baked apple pie that just came out of da oven."

Brandon walked up to Lance and Chuck. "Since Michael has vouched for you and since Carlotta says the spirits have, too, I'll enjoy a slice of her pie. After you finish talking to Danielle, I'll fill you in on what to expect being her bodyguards."

"No." Danielle took a deep breath. "I will tell them about the cartel."

"Cartel?" Lance was ready to do whatever he must to make sure she remained safe.

"The whole story is on page two of WOW," Harry said. "I guess none of you got past the first page."

"Time for dessert, gentlemen." Carlotta's tone was firm.

"I knew this was my lucky day." Michael rubbed his hands together.

Harry shook his head. "Shouldn't we be getting on the road?"

"You're right, honey." Michael turned to Carlotta. "When we get back Monday, can I have some pie then?"

The sweet woman smiled broadly. "Vhy don't I box up a couple of pieces and you and Harry can take dem vith you?"

"Thank you." Michael leaned forward and kissed Carlotta on the cheek. "You're a doll."

"So I've been told many times."

"Danielle, Lance and Chuck are great guys." Michael was a very good friend. "Give them a chance."

"Mmm." Danielle grinned. "Maybe you should start a dating service, Mr. Matchmaker."

"I'd be fantastic at it. Bye. See you on Monday." Michael took the to-go box and left out the front door, Harry following close behind.

"Da spirits are getting restless, Brandon. Lance and Chuck need to ask Danielle a question. To da kitchen. Now."

"I've never been much of a believer in this kind of thing," Lance told the dear lady. "But you're showing me I might need to reconsider."

"That's da spirit."

Carlotta and Brandon went into the kitchen, allowing Lance and Chuck some privacy with the woman he couldn't get enough of.

"Thank you for the flowers, guys. You went a little overboard."

"First things first." Lance wanted to hear the entire story of why she needed bodyguards. "Tell us about the cartel thing."

"It's not as big a deal as everyone is making it."

"Doesn't matter," Chuck stated flatly. "We want to hear everything."

What she told them filled Lance with rage, but he quickly shoved it down. Drug lords weren't to be taken lightly, especially when they thought you had their money. She needed his protection, his and Chuck's, and that was exactly what he was going to give her.

"I want to talk to your sheriff." Lance needed all the details on the cartel. "We have some powerful friends that might be able to help."

"Now, you guys are blowing this up too much. No. I don't want you talking with the sheriff. Please."

"For now, it can wait." He knew Chuck would never wave a white flag of surrender. "But only for now."

"We are taking over being your bodyguards, though." Lance locked his eyes on her. "That's final. No arguments."

"My friend Shelby will appreciate getting her husbands back at home." Danielle smiled. "Okay. It's a deal. For now."

"We're sorry for the trouble we caused yesterday." He grabbed her hand, knowing they'd come on with their old lines. Danielle was more than a conquest to him now. She needed him. He hadn't felt this way about any woman before. Could she be the one for him? For him and Chuck?

Chuck took her other hand. "We got off on the wrong foot. I hope you will forgive us."

"It's fine. You were great. I shouldn't have spilled the tea on you."

"It's settled. We will be your bodyguards going forward." He gazed into her gorgeous eyes. "But will you go out with us?"

* * * *

Danielle knew she shouldn't get involved with anyone because she'd always had to look over her shoulder. *What harm would a single date be?* They were both so handsome, fun, and very nice. "I guess we could go to dinner, if that's all right with you."

"You just made my day." Chuck's sexy, steamy charisma was intoxicating. "Are you working today?"

"Yes. This afternoon is when I start. I won't be getting off until after midnight. I just rushed over here to try to clear things up with Carlotta. Apparently, the spirits beat me to it."

They laughed. She liked the sound of their laughter. It was deep and contagious.

Carlotta walked back into the dining room. "Danielle, I just received a message from the spirits."

That sent her and the two guys into a fit of hysterics.

Her boss smiled. Danielle cared deeply for the woman. "Calm down, children, and listen. Dis is very important."

"Sorry, ma'am." Lance wiped his eyes.

Danielle couldn't get over how easy it was to laugh with him and Chuck. They put her at ease the second she was near them.

"Nothing to be sorry about, young man." Carlotta turned to her. "As I was saying, da spirits came to me and told me to give you da night off. Dey told me it is very important I do dis. And you know vhat else dey told me? I must pay you anyvay."

"Carlotta, I cannot let you do that."

"I have never argued vith da spirits, and I don't intend to start now, young lady."

Chuck turned to Danielle. "Sounds like you are free tonight."

"How about dinner this evening?" Lance asked.

She grinned at Carlotta. "I better not upset the spirits."

"Now you are talking," the woman said. "Go, child. Have fun."

"You were listening at the door, weren't you?"

"Danielle, a psychic never tells her secrets. Professional courtesy, you understand."

Suddenly, the front door opened and in walked two men, carrying more vases of roses in every color imaginable.

"My goodness." Carlotta smiled and shook her head. "Put them with the others, gentlemen." She turned to Lance and Chuck. "Dese men aren't from Vilde."

"No," Chuck answered. "The florist here only had that first batch, but we wanted to send more. So we called the other towns close to here."

"We wanted to impress Danielle," Lance offered.

"A single rose would've done that, guys," she told them, gazing at the roses on the counter. "Thank you. I've never gotten flowers before. And certainly not this many."

"I told you two. A single rose vould've been just fine." Carlotta winked. "You children have fun tonight."

Fun? Danielle had been running from her past for so long she'd never stopped to have fun. "I better get home and get ready for our date. The Horseshoe Bar and Grill has incredible burgers. Or we could eat here."

"Leave the night up to us to plan." Lance squeezed her hand, sending a shiver up and down her spine.

"Okay. Let me say good-bye to Carlotta first. Then we can go." *Time for some fun.* Another shiver rolled through her. *It's only dinner.* She went into the kitchen.

Sitting at the employee table in the back, Brandon was finishing his slice of pie. "Everything okay, Danielle?"

"Relax. I'm fine." She turned to her boss. "Carlotta, I won't argue about tonight, but I will be here for my shift in the morning."

The sweet lady smiled. "Ve vill see how your evening goes before vee decide."

"You're too much. We're going on a date. Dinner. That's the chance they get." She actually was hoping for a wonderful evening with the two sexy men.

Carlotta and Brandon followed her back into the dining room.

"I'm ready to go." She headed to the door.

Brandon leaned against the counter, crossing his arms over his chest. "Take good care of her, fellows."

Lance turned to him. "Absolutely."

Chuck nodded.

They were right behind her as they walked out of the diner.

As she stepped onto the sidewalk, she heard tires screeching.

Looking up, she saw a black sedan heading straight for her.

This is it. This is how I die.

Suddenly, Lance and Chuck pulled her out of the way.

The car swerved back onto Main Street.

Four men were inside, all wielding guns.

One of the bastards threw a brick her direction.

Brandon ran out the door, stopping to fire his gun. He was too late. The car turned onto the highway and sped away.

Chapter Six

Chuck lifted Danielle up in his arms. She was trembling like a leaf. *I just found her and almost lost her.* "Are you alright?"

With her arms around his neck, she nodded. "I'm okay, just a little shaken."

"You're going to be fine. I promise." Lance's face had an air of determination that Chuck hadn't seen in a very long time.

"I'm so glad you both were here." She sighed. "I can't imagine what would've happened if you hadn't been."

Chuck lowered her to her feet, scanning every person and car nearby.

Lance put his arm around her. "We were here, Danielle, and I'm not leaving your side until I can be certain you will be safe." Obviously, his friend was already falling for Danielle, too.

Chuck picked up the brick that had been flung from the car. "There are rubber bands around this. Looks like a note of some kind." He turned to Brandon. "This cartel thing is more serious than I imagined." He freed the piece of paper and held it up. "That was them, right?"

"Without a doubt. Did anyone catch the license plate number?"

"I did, Brandon. It vas an Arizona plate." Carlotta held up a piece of paper. "I vrote it down just now." She handed it to Brandon.

Brandon read the paper. "Quick thinking, Carlotta. Dad can use this."

"I'm not just a pretty face, young man. I've got a brain, too." The woman's voice trembled, clearly trying to shake off what had just happened.

Lance walked up to stand next to Brandon. "Chuck, what does the note say?"

His gut tightened as he read the message. "Dear Ms. Glass, we know you have our money. Consider this a warning. Return what is ours in forty-eight hours or suffer the consequences."

"This is a nightmare." Danielle shook her head, clearly in a state of disbelief. "A total nightmare."

"My God, dey know her name."

Lance grabbed Danielle's hand. "You're not alone in this."

Chuck handed the note to Brandon. "Do you recognize that symbol at the bottom of the page? I've never seen it before."

It was a circle with three lines running vertically through it.

"It's the cartel's calling card. Not sure what it means except it's how they identify their territory. You'll see it on walls, on buildings, and fences throughout the Southwest. We need to go see my dad," Brandon said. "All of us. He'll want to take our statements."

"First, vee take Danielle to Dr. Champion. I vant her checked out thoroughly. She might've hurt herself getting out of da vay of dat car."

"No, Carlotta. Alex spent the entire night in his car outside my place as my bodyguard. He's exhausted. Really, I'm fine." Danielle had a ton of courage, which he couldn't get over. "Because of Lance and Chuck, I'm perfectly fine. I don't want to waste time. I want to get this to Sheriff Champion right now."

Carlotta nodded. "As you vish, child."

Chuck turned to Brandon. "I want to find out everything the sheriff knows."

"And you will. Dad will certainly want to brief you about everything since you and Lance are taking over as Danielle's bodyguards."

Lance put his arm around her. "A slight detour from our plans for tonight, but a necessary one."

"I agree." The worry on her face crushed him.

Chuck touched her on the shoulder. "We will make sure you are safe. I swear."

* * * *

Lance walked into the sheriff's office with Danielle, Chuck, Brandon, and Carlotta.

"Come in," the man behind the desk said. He stood, extending his hand. "I'm Wayne Champion, sheriff of Silver County."

"Lance Archer." He shook his hand. "This is my friend, Chuck Covington. I assume you know the rest."

"I do, especially that good-looking guy over there. They say he looks a lot like his father, you know."

"Dad, we have news," Brandon said. "The cartel just tried to run Danielle over."

The sheriff's smile faded. "Are you okay, young lady?"

"I am."

"You and Carlotta sit. Since there are only two chairs, the guys can stand. I want you all to tell me everything."

Brandon handed him the paper Carlotta had given him. "This is the plate number. The car was a black sedan."

"A four-door Cadillac," Carlotta chimed in. "Late model. I dhink it vas a 2011 or 2012."

"I'll run the plates, but I'm betting they're stolen. That's been the norm."

Lance instantly liked the way Sheriff Champion was getting down to business.

"Look at this, Dad." Brandon handed over the note that had been wrapped around the brick. "I think it's clear who it's from."

"This symbol makes it crystal clear." The sheriff pointed at the note in his hand. "Unfortunately, it's not enough to issue arrest warrants, even if we knew who the men were in the car."

After each of them recounted the event to Sheriff Champion, he leaned back in his chair. "Bastards."

"What I don't understand is why they threw this brick with the note." Danielle shifted in her seat. "Wouldn't it be better from the cartel's point of view to just grab me? Sheriff, why this instead?"

"Intimidation is typical for the cartel. They believe putting the fear of God in a person is the best first move. Most melt. I'm sure they expect you to do the same. Then they don't get their hands dirty with the law."

She folded her arms together. "I won't melt. I promise you that."

Lance liked her grit and determination. But this was most certainly a life and death situation. He didn't want her risking her neck for money. "The cartel wants four hundred thousand. Done. Chuck and I can get that wired to them in a few hours. No problem."

"You can't do that." Danielle's conviction and character was honest. "They're drug dealers and killers. It's not worth it."

"Your safety is worth it to me." *I'd give away my entire fortune to make sure no one harms a single hair on your head, Danielle.*

"She's right," Sheriff Champion said. "You'd only be fuelling an operation that is destroying the lives of kids across most of the western United States. Plus, that would only whet their appetite. Once they find out that you sent the money, they will continue making demands for more. That's how thugs work."

He knew the sheriff was right. "So what other tactic can we take, Sheriff?"

"Do either of you own a gun?"

"We do," Chuck answered. "But they are back at our house in Dallas."

"If you're going to be Danielle's new bodyguards, we'll have to get you armed."

"How good are you two vith guns?" Carlotta asked.

"Actually, we're quite good. Chuck and I have won our share of medals at the gun range."

Brandon shrugged. "A paper target doesn't move, Lance."

"I'm really good at skeet shooting. They move."

The sheriff laughed, breaking the tension slightly. The rest joined in, allowing everyone a chance to breathe.

"Men," the sheriff said, "Danielle's got her own gun."

Lance looked at her, shocked at the revelation. "Is that true?"

She nodded. "Everyone in Wilde has a gun."

"I don't want her to use it—ever," Sheriff Champion stated firmly. "She shouldn't have to, if you do your jobs."

"As her bodyguards, I swear we will make sure she is safe." Lance looked at Chuck and saw the same determination in his face.

"Sheriff, do you have a gun store here?" Chuck asked.

A knock on the door startled all of them.

Sheriff Champion stood.

Brandon's hand went inside his jacket.

He and Chuck jumped in front of Danielle and Carlotta to block them from whoever might come through the door.

"Sheriff, it's Austin Wilde. I've got news."

He saw Brandon's hand return to his side and the sheriff sighed, which made everyone relax.

"Come in," the sheriff said.

The man walked into the office. He had a bearing of authority that couldn't be missed.

"Austin, I'd like you to meet Lance Archer and Chuck Covington. They will be Danielle's acting bodyguards."

They shook hands.

"What's the news?" Brandon asked.

"Someone has approached the cartel about Danielle," Austin stated. "A guy who just got out of prison. Quite the rap sheet, too. Burglar and con artist turned drug dealer. Name of Miguel Soto."

Danielle's face turned white, but she didn't say a word.

Austin continued. "He was in for murder. What I've drummed up so far on the guy is he contacted the cartel for their resources. Made some big promises to them. You know anything about him?" he asked

Danielle.

She didn't answer.

Lance saw a look on her face that didn't sit well with him. She was afraid.

The sheriff looked at Danielle like a father would a daughter. "Honey, don't worry. We'll investigate this." He turned to Austin. "What else?"

"Whatever Soto told the cartel about Danielle must've worked. They seem more excited about Danielle than ever before."

"The pieces of the puzzle are starting to come together." Sheriff Champion filled Austin in on what had happened outside of Norma's Diner. "It's very clear who is after her."

He handed the brick and note to Austin.

Austin read the note. His gaze returned to Danielle. "Any light you can shed on this or on who Soto is?"

"You already asked her that," Lance shot at him. "Back off."

The man's hands curled into fists. Didn't matter. If they had to come to blows, so be it. Lance's need to protect Danielle was so massive inside him. He would do whatever necessary to make sure she remained safe—not just from the cartel's thugs or this Soto guy, but even from Austin's unspoken accusations, if need be.

"Hold on, men," the sheriff said calmly. "Let's table this. I'm in charge of this investigation."

"Look, Sheriff. I'm only trying to help her," Austin stated. "The more I know, the more I can do for her. We all want the same thing. We want Danielle to be safe."

Hearing that and seeing the man's hands relax made Lance feel better about Austin.

"What about Trent?" The concern in Danielle's voice was unmistakable.

"I spoke with Masters just a few minutes ago," Austin said. "Trent isn't crazy about being assigned bodyguards."

"Can't blame him." She smiled, turning to him and Chuck. "It could be worse."

The man's face darkened. "You're damn right it could be."

"Too bad," the sheriff stated. "Until I say so, both Danielle and Trent will have protective detail around them at all times. How's Trent holding up?"

"After the hell he went through, better than most. The guy is tough."

Brandon nodded. "Coming from you, Austin, that's saying a lot."

"Trent is tough like his sister, Mackenzie." The sheriff turned to him and Chuck. "Time to take you to the gun store."

"Past time." Chuck's tone had a steely edge he'd heard a million times. It was time to get to the job at hand—protecting Danielle.

Lance put his arm around her shoulder. "We're taking you on a date."

Chuck nodded. "Tonight."

The sheriff reached for his keys and began walking toward the door. "After we get you two pistols, of course. A date might be good for you, Danielle."

Lance touched her cheek. "We'll stay sharp and remain on guard, but I want to get your mind off of this mess."

"That would be great," she said, her eyes wide. "I need a break from all of this."

Chapter Seven

As she unlocked the door to her house, Danielle's insides whirled like mad. She led Lance and Chuck inside. Each of them had guns holstered inside their jackets. Lance had a Glock and Chuck had a .45 magnum.

Miguel is coming for me.

"I love your place." Chuck's gaze wandered around her home. Lance smiled. "It fits you, Danielle."

"But you just met me."

"I know, but it goes along with your sweet personality." He held her hand. "There are clues all over the place about who you are, especially in your decorations."

Chuck put his arm around her. "Comfortable and welcoming."

She was glad that he and Chuck were here. She didn't want to be alone. Not after learning from Austin that Soto was trying to track her down. How many years had it been since she'd seen the asshole? Not since she was twelve, so ten years.

Ten years. God, has it really been that long?

"I know you want to take me on a date, but do you mind if we just sit for a bit before I get ready?"

"Don't mind at all." Lance touched her cheek. "If you'd rather stay in than go out, we can."

"I agree." Chuck pulled her in tighter to his muscled frame. "You're tough, Danielle, but anyone would need some time to get over what happened to you outside the diner."

"Thank you. Would either of you like something to drink?"

"Let's just sit on your sofa for now," Lance said. "Take a breather from everything we heard in the sheriff's office."

"Thanks, I believe that's exactly what I need." She sat on her sofa and touched Pauline's book to try to calm her nerves. "I still can't believe you are doing this for me."

"You heard Michael." Chuck smiled. "We're good guys."

"I believe you are." She closed her eyes, trying to push the ancient nightmare down. It wouldn't go back into the cage now that she knew Miguel was searching for her.

"It's going to be okay, Danielle." The tenderness in Lance's voice was comforting.

She wanted to believe him, needed to. But she couldn't. Nothing was going to be okay again. She opened her eyes and looked at the book dear Pauline had given her.

"You're a good person, too." Chuck's face was full of compassion. "I can tell."

"Can you? I don't feel so good." Lance and Chuck had agreed to be her bodyguards. The least they deserved was to know the truth. "I'm not who you think I am. My last name isn't even Glass. I lied. I've been lying for so long, sometimes I wonder if I even know the truth."

"Danielle, there has to be a reason for you to use another name." Chuck seemed to be as much of a mind reader as Carlotta was a psychic. "I'm a great judge of character. I know I'm right."

"What is your last name, sweetheart?" Lance asked.

"Roberson. I'm Danielle Roberson." It felt good to tell them her real name. Now three people in Wilde knew it—*Lance, Chuck, and the sheriff.*

Chuck put his arm around her. "You can trust us to know your truth. It will not leave this room."

"Whatever happened to you, we're here for you, Danielle." Lance's gaze made her melt. "You can count on us."

"Where to begin?" She took a deep breath as the memories filled her mind. "My dad died when I was five years old. My mother lost it.

She wasn't the mom I remembered, the mom who tucked me in at night, the mom who made sure I was clean and fed, the mom who read stories to me before I went to sleep. I was an only child and so it was just my mother and I for a couple of years. My mother started drinking and fell into a bad crowd. She went from one man to the next for a couple of years before settling on a burglar, who she married when I was seven. Miguel Soto is my stepfather."

Lance held her hand and squeezed. "My God, no wonder you got so upset when Austin mentioned his name."

"So how did he end up in prison?" Chuck asked.

"Murder, but it's a very long story and I want to tell you." She looked at them both and saw such kindness in their eyes. It made it easier to talk to them, to tell them her truth. "Soto could pick any lock, but he grew tired of robbery. He and my mother started a scam against elderly people. I was too young to know what was going on. They worked as home health aides. They would gain their clients' trust and steal small amounts from them. In time, they would coerce their victims to sign over their assets."

"That's horrible, Danielle." Lance squeezed her hand.

"Posing as a handyman and housekeeper, they brought me into the scam, though I still had no idea they were criminals. My mom told me to talk to the elderly people because they were lonely and loved children. I had no grandparents, so I was thrilled to do it. Later, I realized my mom and Miguel were only using me. They believed their victims would see me as a sweet, innocent child. They were right. We looked just like a loving family, so they opened up their hearts and wallets for us."

Chuck's eyes narrowed. "How could they use a child for their dirty work?"

"If the elderly people would ask my mother or Miguel questions about what they were doing, then the bastard would give me a spanking at night, saying I wasn't doing my job keeping them occupied. My mother never did anything to protect me."

"I'd like to get my hands on your fucking stepfather." Lance's face was full of rage.

"Every night I would cry myself to sleep." She leaned back, feeling the weight of the past crushing into her gut. "I was twelve years old when we started working for Mrs. Pauline Laddell. She gave me this on the day she died." Danielle pointed to the book on the coffee table. "It's my most prized possession. Pauline loved to read to me. I fell in love with books because of her. She was the sweetest woman I'd ever known. We talked for hours and hours about all kinds of things. We baked cookies together. She told me about her life with her husband, Ernest, who had been a Navy pilot. They'd lived all around the world. I loved her very much."

"So she was like a grandmother to you?" Chuck asked.

"Most definitely. After handing me the book, Pauline sent me into the kitchen to get her a cup of tea. I held my present to my chest. No one had ever given me anything. Ever."

Lance shook his head. "Not even for your birthday?"

"Not even then. Pauline's gift was the only one I'd ever received." Danielle closed her eyes and brought up the vision of that horrible day. "When I walked into the kitchen, I saw my mother putting one of Pauline's silver trays into her bag. I'd seen my mother do that kind of thing many times, but she'd always have some kind of reason why, like needing to get something repaired or cleaned. For many years, I accepted everything she told me. But growing into my adolescence and turning twelve, I realized it had been lies all along. I'd been so foolish."

"You were only a child, sweetheart." Chuck patted her tenderly.

"I had to tell Pauline. I turned to go to her, but Miguel grabbed me. I'll never forget how evil his eyes looked that day. He bent down and said, 'What are you doing, you little fuck? Don't you dare tell that bitch anything. You do and you die, and so does Pauline. Understand?' He saw the book and his lips curled into a twisted smile. 'The fruit doesn't fall far from the tree, Danielle. Nice little treasure you lifted.' I told him that Pauline had given me the book, and I tried to wiggle free from his hold. But he held me tight."

"Motherfucker," Lance cursed through clenched teeth.

"That's when he told me what the scam was and what my job had been for all those dear people we'd stolen from. I'll never forget his words that day. 'Everything in this house is mine, Danielle, including this book. You're worthless. You don't deserve anything, you little bitch.' I cried. I saw my mother, but like always, she didn't take a single step to save me. He cursed and shoved me in a closet, threatening to cut my throat if I moved a muscle. He shut the door and I shook violently. When I caught my breath, I bolted out of the closet. Miguel stood behind Pauline. She smiled at me. And then Miguel swung a lamp at the dear woman's head."

"Oh my God," they both said in unison.

With tears of grief welling up in her eyes, she continued. "As Pauline's body fell to the ground, I ran out the door and down the street. I kept running. I ran as fast as I could. I didn't look back. I knew I couldn't go back. Not to him. Not even to my mother. Pauline was dead. He'd killed her. That first night, behind a dumpster, I cried myself to sleep."

Lance and Chuck held her close.

"Even though I'd been in the dark about the cons Miguel and my mom had run, I had learned how to survive growing up with them. Because of their selfishness and neglect, I had to. I hitched a ride to Los Angeles, thinking they wouldn't be able to find me in such a big city. Even though I was only twelve, I got a job waiting tables, claiming to be sixteen. That's when all the lies and running started."

Lance kissed her. "You don't have to run anymore."

"We'll make sure you don't." Chuck stroked her hair.

"I like it here. I like being with you two. I ended up in Wilde because of the stories Pauline told me about it. She grew up here as a child. The way she talked about that time sounded incredible. All those years of running, I never forgot them. Now, I'm here."

"With us." Lance smiled. "This town does seem special."

"We've only been here a couple of days, but I completely agree, buddy."

She grabbed their hands, feeling better than she had in her entire life. Pauline was right. "Wilde is like no other place on the planet."

Chuck kissed her neck. "And you're like no other woman I've ever known."

Tingles spread through her body. She turned her head to him, inviting his lips to take hers.

Their kiss began tenderly, deepening to hot passion until her toes curled and her breath caught in her chest.

She felt Lance stroke her hair. Turning to him, she saw his soft, loving eyes lock in on her. She wanted his lips on hers, too, just like they'd been in the dream.

As if he'd read her mind, he pressed his mouth to hers, delivering a shiver up and down her spine. It felt so good to really let go. She'd had to be tough and guarded for so long. Unlike her, they had experience with sex that was evident with every kiss and caress. The more they touched her, the more her body responded. She wanted this, wanted it with all her heart. They were wonderful men and had been so good to her. She'd trusted them with her secrets. Couldn't she trust them with more? Deep inside, she wanted to.

As Lance's tongue slipped past her lips, Chuck gently reached under her blouse and bra and massaged her breasts. Feeling his hands on her skin raised her desires beyond anything she'd ever experienced. *No one has ever touched me there.*

Lance slipped off the sofa and knelt in front of her between her thighs. She watched him unbutton her pants. "You're beautiful, Danielle. You're the most beautiful creature I've ever seen." Slowly, he slipped her slacks down, exposing her pale pink thong.

Oh God. This feels so good.

Chuck's thumbs grazed her nipples, causing them to tighten and tingle.

Lance pulled her thong down to her knees, and she saw his eyes widen and a smile spread across his face. He bent down and dotted kisses on her inner thighs, moving ever so slowly closer to her pussy.

Her insides burned hot, reaching deep into her core. She wanted them so very much, but she must let them know she'd never been with anyone. Ever.

She took a deep breath. "Stop."

Lance and Chuck looked at her with surprise, their eyes full of questions.

"What's wrong, baby?" Chuck asked.

Lance leaned back. "Are we coming on to strong?"

"No. It's just that I must tell you something."

"Go on, sweetheart." Chuck's face softened with concern. "We're here for you."

"It's just that I've never…um…"

"Never what, Danielle?" Lance asked.

Here it goes. Time to let them know the whole truth. "I've never been with anyone. No one has ever touched me before. I'm afraid I'll disappoint you." She couldn't bear to look at them and lowered her eyes.

Chuck touched her cheek. "You could never disappoint us, baby."

She looked at him and saw such compassion and warmth.

Lance grabbed her hands. "You are beautiful, charming, sexy, sweet, and everything else any man would want."

She turned to him and saw the same measure of goodness she'd seen in Chuck. *How was I so lucky to have these two come into my life?*

Lance continued. "God knows I want you, but if you're not ready for this then I will wait."

"Same here," Chuck agreed.

"I want you more than anything," she confessed. "I just need to know how you feel about me being a virgin."

Both of them smiled broadly.

Lance spoke first. "I think it's so wonderful that we will be your first."

Chuck nodded. "We definitely don't want to disappoint you."

"How could you? You were already making me feel so special."

"You've done the same for us, baby." Lance was so sexy and understanding.

"We're both overwhelmed and honored that you trust us with this most precious gift." Chuck kissed her and she melted into him.

She could feel Lance's hot, manly breath on her pussy. His mouth hovered above her mound as he gently massaged her thighs. Her need multiplied with every beat of her racing heart. She'd waited for this night for so long in the hopes she would find someone who would give her an experience she would never forget. *I found two someones, or did they find me?*

"Lift your legs for me, baby," Lance said.

She did, and he pulled her pants and thong the rest of the way off. Chuck removed her top and bra, leaving her completely exposed. *This feels so natural, so right.*

He and Lance removed their clothes in a flash. Seeing their naked bodies delighted her. She'd never seen a man in the flesh, face-to-face, in living color. Unable to resist, her eyes went down to their cocks, which were enormous and already erect.

She gasped. "You're both so big. Is that normal?"

They chuckled.

"Honey, Lance is slightly above average, whereas I'm way above," Chuck teased.

Lance shot his friend his happy middle finger. "She can see for herself, buddy, who is bigger."

She needed to stop this before it got out of hand. "You look about the same to me. I've always heard size doesn't matter."

Chuck's hungry eyes were enticing. "We'll let you decide, baby."

"How would I know? You're going to be my first."

Lance smiled. "You'll just know, sweetheart."

Her eyes drank in their muscles. "You are both so gorgeous."

Lance's gaze moved up and down her body. "I've never seen a more beautiful woman in all my life."

Chuck's eyes were full of desire. "You are perfection, baby."

Lance bent down and pulled out some condoms from his front pocket, handing one to Chuck.

My God, I didn't even think about protection. I'm glad they did. She liked that they were in control.

Like a woman entranced, she watched them open the foil packages and roll rubbers down their long, thick cocks. Even that little display heightened her excitement.

She needed them to touch her. "I want you both now."

Chuck grinned. "Not so fast, sweetheart."

Lance lifted her up in his arms. "Trust us, baby. Let us be in control, and we will make sure you have the best night of your life."

"I do trust you. I trust both of you." She wrapped her arms around his neck, relishing the feel of his naked body on her skin.

He carried her into her bedroom with Chuck right behind.

Chuck pulled off the comforter from her bed, and Lance lowered her to the mattress.

She felt their hands roaming on her body, causing her temperature to rise higher and higher.

Chuck sucked on her nipples, creating a line of tingling sensations that went from her breasts all the way down to her sex.

Lance moved between her legs, his lips a fraction of an inch from her dampening pussy.

"Please, Lance. Please."

She felt his fingers thread through her folds, sending a wanton shock through her entire body. When he kissed her mound, she fisted the sheets. The dream had been like no other, but now, being with them here, on her bed, in their arms, was so real, so intense, so passionate.

Everything inside her exploded. Her body was responding in ways she'd never experienced before. With Lance's mouth on her pussy and Chuck's on her breast, she writhed on the mattress. Her vibrator had never given her this kind of orgasm.

"Oh God. Yes." Sensations soared through every fiber of her being. She couldn't control her body. It had a mind of its own, shaking violently from head to toe.

Lance and Chuck caressed her tenderly as her trembles subsided ever so slightly.

"I'm going to take you now, sweetheart." Lance crawled up her body until she could feel his cock pressing on her pussy. "It will sting for a moment but I will be gentle."

Chuck lifted her up slightly and moved behind her on the bed. She rested against his chest as he whispered in her ear. "Just go with it, baby. Feel the intimacy we are sharing."

"I'm so ready. I want this more than anything."

Lance smiled and pressed his mouth to hers. As he intensified their kiss, she felt the tip of his cock slip into her pussy, taking her breath away. She clutched his back as he slowly went into her body.

His unblinking eyes held her captive. "Take a deep breath for me, baby."

She did and she felt him thrust his cock into her pussy, delivering a sharp sting. Lance froze in place, his dick deep inside her, capturing her with his eyes, which were full of kindness and concern.

"Breathe, honey," Chuck's hands massaged her breasts, driving her crazy.

Not realizing she was holding her breath, she let out a lungful of air.

The pain quickly subsided and transformed into something new, something strong, something amazing—an overpowering need. She had wanted them more than anything she'd ever wanted in her life. Now her dream was coming true.

"Yes. God yes," she panted over and over.

Lance renewed his thrusts into her body, sending his cock deeper into her burning flesh. He began to go faster, and she wrapped her legs around his back, desiring all of him.

Her body kept climbing into a state of dizzy passion. "Oh, Lance."

"Come for us, baby," Chuck whispered in her ear. "Feel every cell in your body on fire."

Like a match to a fuse, his words and Lance's thrusts sent her over the edge into a sea of release. So many sensations rolled through her, each more powerful than the one before.

Lance's gaze locked in on her, but the passion in his eyes could not be missed. "I'm going to come."

One last deep plunge of Lance's cock into her pussy and she felt his body stiffen above her. He groaned and his eyes closed. Her body responded, tightening on his shaft again and again as he shot his seed.

He let out a long sigh, and the weight of his spent body pinned her to the mattress.

Chuck kissed her. "That was so beautiful, sweetheart. How are you?"

"Amazing," she confessed. "I want you, Chuck. I want you now."

"I want you, too."

Lance rolled to the side, pulling his cock out of her pussy.

Immediately, Chuck moved from behind her and took his place, plunging his dick into her depths.

The pressure returned with every thrust into her body. "Yes, Chuck. Yes."

Her insides tightened around his shaft, clenching and unclenching again and again. She felt alive and on fire.

"Fuuuck," Chuck moaned, sending his cock deep into her in one final thrust.

Feeling him inside her, she climaxed, vibrating from head to toe. Happy tears welled up in her eyes. She felt so connected to them. She would never forget this night, not in a million years.

It took some time for her body to settle down and return to normal. Lance and Chuck held her close, caressing her.

Her stomach roared. "I'm starving. Does sex make you hungry?"

They both laughed.

"Honey, look what time it is." Chuck pointed to the clock on her nightstand.

"I had no idea it was past seven."

"It's been a busy day." Lance's stomach growled audibly, as if on cue.

She giggled. "You sound like you are starving, too."

"We never stopped for lunch after we left the sheriff's office."

"We had to buy our guns." Chuck grinned. "We took a little longer than we should have, I guess."

Lance stroked her hair. "Speaking of guns. Which one of us is the largest, Danielle?"

Chuck nodded. "Time for you to have a reality check, buddy. Tell him, baby."

She leaned up and kissed them both. "The truth is, of all the men I've been with, you two are the largest."

They all burst into laughter.

"If you're going to dodge that bullet, tell us who shoots the fastest?" Chuck teased.

"I wasn't looking at the clock." She grinned. "Were either of you?"

They both shook their heads.

Lance looked at his friend. "She's going to be trouble, Chuck. The kind of trouble we both like, don't you think?"

"I definitely do," Chuck agreed. "What would you like to eat, sweetheart?"

She didn't even have to think about that. "I would love a cheeseburger. You're going to like the Horsehoe Bar and Grill. She makes the best burgers in the whole state."

"How about a shower first?" Lance asked, his eyes gleaming.

Chuck smiled. "You read my mind, buddy."

They were scheming again. She just knew it. "Why do I get the feeling this isn't just about cleaning up?"

"Because you can read our minds, too, baby." Lance lifted her off the bed. "Dinner will have to wait."

They took her into the bathroom, and she felt happier than she had in her entire life.

Chapter Eight

With the morning sun coming in through the window, Chuck kissed Danielle. He still couldn't believe how lucky he and Lance were to be here with her.

Danielle's eyes fluttered open. "What time is it?"

Lance yawned and picked up his Rolex from the nightstand. "Eight-thirty."

"I started a bath for you, Danielle." He kissed her again, enjoying the softness of her lips. "I want you to get in and soak while Lance and I rustle up some food for us."

She stretched her arms over her head. "I need to help you cook."

Lance gave her a quick kiss on the forehead. "I'm with Chuck on this, darlin'. You have eggs?"

"Yes."

"Bacon or sausage?"

"Both."

"Breakfast is my favorite meal." Lance wasn't lying. Once he'd devoured three stacks of pancakes in one sitting back in college. "We can handle ourselves fine in your kitchen. You just relax."

"Are you sure?" She grinned, making her look even more beautiful. "I don't want you two thinking I'm lazy. Besides, you're my guests, not the other way around."

"You. Bath. Us. Kitchen." Chuck brushed the hair out of her eye. "That's final."

He lifted her off the mattress.

She wrapped her arms around his neck. "I can walk, you know."

He loved the feel of her body next to his. "I am sure you can, but I want to give you five-star treatment."

"Is this what they do at those fancy hotels you and Lance stay at? Carry you to the bathroom?"

He laughed. When they came to the tub, he lowered her into the warm water.

The smile that spread across her face thrilled him. "The temperature is perfect. Just right."

Lance came in with a glass of wine, a cup of coffee and a candle. "I couldn't decide which beverage you would prefer, so I brought both. I thought something to drink and a candle might enhance the experience for you, baby."

"It's 8:30 in the morning. Coffee might be more appropriate, but I think wine is perfect. Thank you."

Chuck folded up a plush towel and placed it behind her head. "Just relax, Danielle. We'll be within shouting distance if you need anything at all."

"As small as my place is, I bet I could whisper and you would hear me, even in the kitchen."

He bent down and pressed his lips to hers, relishing the taste of her. "Your place is perfect."

"This must look like a matchbox compared to your homes."

Lance shook his head. "This is the most beautiful place I've seen in my life."

Chuck thought about all the houses they had around the world. None would compare to the warmth he felt here at Danielle's place.

* * * *

Staring at the flame of the candle, Danielle sipped on the wine.

Chuck and Lance had made love to her after hearing her story. God, she'd never felt so safe in all her life. They'd made it clear they would protect her. It was more than just feeling safe to her. She felt so comfortable with them.

From their very first introduction, she'd been able to laugh freely. Now, she could cry openly and show her anger, fear, and true self without pretense. She'd never done that with anyone. The sheriff knew most of her history, but Lance and Chuck now knew everything. Her name. Her past. All of it. And they still wanted her. And she wanted them. That was the truth.

Where is this going? I don't know, but I'm enjoying what we have now.

When she heard Lance and Chuck laughing in her kitchen, she thought it might be time to dry off and go help them. *But I still have half a glass of wine.*

She giggled. It seemed so funny that Lance and Chuck, who likely had a staff at their beck and call to meet their every need and whim, were in her tiny kitchen, right now, making her breakfast. *I must be the luckiest woman in the world.*

Am I dreaming again? I am naked. She laughed, expecting to hear elephants off in the distance. *Oh my God, will I ever be able to go to a zoo again without getting all hot and bothered?* She grinned and took another sip.

Lance and Chuck had told her to enjoy her bath.

Why not soak a little longer?

* * * *

Lance stood over the stove, listening to the sizzle of the bacon. His stomach growled in response, but all his thoughts were on Danielle, who was still in the bathtub.

His Glock was on the counter within reach.

Chuck's weapon was holstered to his side. He started a second pot of coffee. "This reminds me of the early days. Back in our first apartment."

"I know. Ramen noodles and beer. That got us through several lean months."

"There were quite a few of them, but we sure had fun."

"As I recall, I was the best cook." Lance never tired of talking about the old days when he and Chuck had worked hard to build up their company. It had been the best time of his life. "You burned everything. Even popcorn."

"The power on that microwave was much stronger than it should've been and you know it."

"True, but I adjusted the cook time to account for it. Hence, perfect kernels every time."

They both laughed.

"Seriously, buddy." Chuck smiled. "I can't remember having this much fun, ever."

"Me either." Their college days were great, but this was different. "It's because of her, you know."

"Damn right it is. She's amazing."

"We need to talk to the sheriff about Soto. He needs to know everything." Lance felt his pulse get hot, realizing how awful Danielle's young life had been. "I'd also like to bring in more help. We can hire the best to find the fucker. I don't want him anywhere near her."

"I completely agree." Chuck put some plates on the table. "I like her, Lance. I like her very much."

"So do I." He and Chuck were on the same page, and that thrilled him. Now, they could move things forward with Danielle. "I've never met anyone who holds a candle to her. After everything she's gone through, she just keeps on going. Most would've crawled into a hole and given up."

"She's so funny and beautiful." Chuck's tone held a reverence and awe. Like him, Chuck was completely mesmerized by Danielle. "God, listen to us, buddy. We sound like two lovesick school boys."

"I know." *Is that what we are? Lovesick?*

* * * *

Danielle looked at her fingertips, which were wrinkled beyond belief. Her glass of wine was empty and the candle had burned down. The water, which had been very hot, was now cool.

How long have I been in here? Quite long, by the looks of things.

She stood and grabbed a towel.

Drying off, she smelled the aroma of bacon.

After putting on a robe, she walked into the kitchen. Lance and Chuck both gave her a kiss and led her to the table, which was filled with a delicious meal of scrambled eggs, bacon, hash browns, and biscuits and gravy.

"This is quite the breakfast you've prepared, gentlemen. Thank you. I rarely eat at home since I work at the diner. This is very nice."

Chuck put his arm around her. "Our pleasure, sweetheart."

Lance pulled the chair out for her, and she took a seat.

"You two are spoiling me."

"That's the plan." Lance's sweet side was something she couldn't get enough of. "Do you feel better after your bath?"

"I do. Very relaxed." She took a bite of bacon, which was cooked just to her liking. Crispy. "Delicious."

"Try the orange juice." Chuck's gentle strength was intoxicating. "That was my contribution."

"He pours like a pro, Danielle," Lance teased. "I can't wait for you to taste the gravy. My mother was an incredible cook. She taught me how to make it."

"No time like the present." She took a big fluffy biscuit and broke it in two. She covered the pieces in Lance's cream gravy. She took a forkful and brought it to her mouth. It tasted fantastic. "This is the best gravy I've ever had. You have to share your recipe with Carlotta and the cooks. It would be a huge hit." She took another bite.

Lance smiled. "I knew you would like it."

They finished the meal, laughing and talking. It felt so natural being with Lance and Chuck. They didn't come off as rich bastards.

She believed they could fit in anywhere, here at her kitchen table as well as boardrooms at corporations. Their charm and confidence was so appealing.

"Guys, I want to go see the sheriff." Sharing everything with Lance and Chuck had opened her up to trust. Sheriff Champion deserved to hear the rest of her story. "He knows some of what I told you, but I need to tell him the rest."

The sheriff knew her real name and knew about Miguel and her mom. What she hadn't told him was how really bad it was growing up with those two. He needed to hear all of it. Maybe in some way that would help him and Austin in their mission to bring down the cartel and save not just her, but also poor Trent.

"Sheriff Champion is a good man. Yes, you need to tell him everything." Lance grabbed her hand and squeezed. "What time do you want to get to his office?"

"My shift starts at two this afternoon, so at least by noon."

"I don't think you need to be working right now." Chuck's tone was stern. "We need to keep our eyes on you."

She smiled. "Overprotective looks good on you, Mr. Covington. I'll be fine at the diner. You can stay there if you want for my whole shift, but I doubt the cartel would make a move in broad daylight in such a public place with so many people."

"Don't forget about the car that nearly ran you over, honey." Lance looked quite serious. "That was broad daylight, too."

"You're right, but I can't let Carlotta down. She's done so much for me."

Lance cleared the dishes. "We'll make sure she's not left hanging."

"We'll take care of it." Chuck wiped the table. God, she enjoyed being pampered by him and Lance. "But I do agree with you that you need to talk to the sheriff again. We'll get you there safe and sound."

She stood to help finish cleaning up the meal, but both of them motioned for her to stay put. Their take-charge demeanors spoke to her deeply. *They're quite the duo.* She couldn't help but like them, and the truth was, she could feel her heart warming even more to them every second she was with them.

"I'm going to check the perimeter, Chuck." Lance grabbed his gun, reminding her how dangerous her current situation was.

"I'll stay with Danielle, but we'll make sure all the locks on the windows and doors are secure."

If Miguel did find her, with the help of the cartel, at least she wouldn't be alone. She would be with Lance and Chuck, her bodyguards. Knowing that made her feel a little better, but she prayed the bastard would never find her. The chances she wouldn't have to face him were slim. The cartel was helping Miguel. Why? What lies had he told them about her to enlist their aid?

An image of her mother floated in the back of her mind. Had she gone to prison, too? Where was she? Was her mother with Miguel still? She'd never bothered to check, trying to completely separate herself from that life.

* * * *

Miguel Soto parked the Harley he'd stolen two days ago in front of the coin-op Laundromat. He walked in and looked at the man behind the desk. He'd been one of the few trusted friends of Miguel's before he'd gone to prison.

"Hey, Soliz."

"Miguel, I'm glad you got out. All the old gang heard about your call to your cousin."

"Yeah. That's why I'm here. To see Ricardo."

Soliz smiled. "He's expecting you."

"I heard things had changed."

"Some good and some bad, Miguel. Your cousin is top of the food chain these days." Soliz shrugged and then leaned forward. "Everyone will be glad to see you."

"I've got some business to attend to, but tell them I will be contacting them soon."

"Just like the old days. *Perfecto*. I think you'll like what we've done for you while you were away." The man looked around and whispered. "You have many supporters."

"You're a true friend, Soliz." Miguel walked to the door, passing the women who were folding their clothes. Several young children were running around. One nearly knocked into him. If he'd been somewhere else, he wouldn't have thought twice to kick the little bastard. But Gomez Washateria was just another front for the Rio Grande cartel, which controlled all the trafficking in the entire Southwest, so he plastered a smile on his face.

He looked at the sign on the door, which read "Employees Only." He pushed it open and came face-to-face with two men carrying assault rifles, neither of whom he recognized. *Ricardo's men.*

"*Manos a la cabeza*," the taller of the two ordered.

He complied, placing his hands on his head. They frisked him and removed his pistol.

They led him to another door. The shorter man knocked.

"Come." A voice he hadn't heard in years came through the door.

They opened it and he walked in and saw Ricardo Delgado, the *capo* of the most powerful cartel in the States. "*Hola*, cousin."

"Hello, Ricardo. I'm glad to be talking to you instead of your underlings."

"Business keeps me busy, Miguel. Sit."

He took a seat.

"As you know, much has happened since you went to prison." Ricardo motioned to the two men who had escorted him here, and they left the room. "You and I don't have much family left, Miguel. My father is dead. Carlos took over, but was gunned down shortly after. Your father is dead. Family is family. Now that you are out, I'd like to offer you a job in my organization."

"Your organization?" The bastard was more smug than he

remembered him to be. "I know Carlos is dead, but you and I are equals. That hasn't changed."

"You went to prison, Miguel. Everything has changed." Ricardo picked up the phone. "Send her in."

"Do you have my stepdaughter or not?"

"Straight to business. I like that." Ricardo leaned back in his chair. "My men sent her a message. We'll see how she responds."

He frowned. "You just want me to sit back and wait?"

"That's exactly what you will do, Miguel. What I want. This town she lives in has been problematic to the organization. Patience has gotten me to this chair. No one will harm Danielle unless I give the order. Trust me. We wait."

The door opened and Merle, Miguel's wife and Danielle's mother, walked in. Miguel hadn't expected to see her again. She'd refused to testify on his behalf in the murder case.

Fucking bitch. What was she doing here?

"Ah, my pet." Ricardo smiled, letting Miguel know the score. Merle was with his cousin now. This was Ricardo's way of reminding him who was in charge. "Come over here and give your man a kiss."

Miguel's gut tightened in rage, but he remained silent, knowing his cousin had all the cards stacked in his favor at the moment. *The cunt is mine, bastard.* He thought about Soliz's earlier words. Time to plan a takeover. He couldn't wait to put a bullet in Ricardo's head.

Merle looked as beautiful as he remembered, though her eyes were vacant. She glanced at him and sighed. She went to his cousin, who grabbed her and pulled her into his lap. He kissed her, not with passion but with a sign of his power.

Fucker.

"You're the boss." His gut burned with hate.

"Cousin, we have a common interest in Danielle, but I want to know more about this treasure she stole from you."

He wasn't going to tell him about the book. "Jewels. Merle, you remember Pauline, don't you?"

She nodded meekly.

What a whore Merle was. She would pay. Ricardo would pay. Danielle would pay.

All he needed was the book.

Chapter Nine

At 11:45 am, Danielle walked into Sheriff Champion's office with Lance and Chuck.

"Good morning." The sheriff sat behind his desk. "Have a seat."

"Sheriff, Chuck and I are headed to the diner," Lance said. "One of us will be taking Danielle's shift today. The other will be back to pick her up when she's done talking to you."

"I told you that I am fully capable of working my shift, guys. As much as I appreciate all you're doing for me, you don't have to do this."

Chuck placed a firm hand on her shoulder. "With the cartel and Soto gunning for you, it's best for you to keep your head down and stay out of sight."

"I'm surprised you let me out of my house, guys. I feel like I'm under house arrest."

Sheriff Champion's eyes narrowed. "Young lady, you need to listen to them. They're right about this. We need to be very cautious when it comes to you. I'm glad that Lance and Chuck realize how serious this is. You almost got run over by a car yesterday, or have you forgotten?"

Thrilled with Wayne Champion's fatherly demeanor, she smiled. "I haven't forgotten. Do you really think they would try something like that again? Inside the diner?"

"Danielle, the cartel is unpredictable," the sheriff said.

Chuck kissed her gently. "We can't be too careful."

She looked over at the sheriff, who sent her a knowing wink. "Three against one. You win. I'll stay away from the diner. But you better do your best for Carlotta, guys. Whichever one of you ends up working my shift today, work hard. Okay?"

"That'll be me, and I will." Lance kissed her. "Chuck is taking your shift tomorrow."

They walked out the door, leaving her alone with Sheriff Champion.

He smiled. "Very nice guys, those two."

"Yes, they are." God, meeting Lance and Chuck had been the best thing to happen to her in a long time.

Was she playing with fire? Would her heart get burned if she kept going down this path? Probably, but good or bad, she wanted to spend more time with Lance and Chuck.

"Danielle, I can see you have feelings for them, don't you?"

She'd expected that out of Carlotta. But the sheriff? "Is everyone in Wilde tasked with playing matchmaker?"

He laughed. "I suppose so."

"We only just met, Sheriff."

"Not a big believer in love at first sight? I am. The second I saw Connie, I knew she was for me. She's the love of my life, my dream girl. Seeing how those two fellows are with you, I think they have already fallen for you, too."

She wouldn't mind being Lance and Chuck's dream girl. "You're a hopeless romantic, Sheriff."

"I am. Completely hopeless. Mark my words, Danielle. You three belong together."

She wished he was right, but she knew she came with a ton of baggage. Was that fair to Lance and Chuck? They had little of their own. Their lives seemed so perfect. Billionaire bachelors. How could she ever fit in?

"I want to talk to you about Miguel Soto, Sheriff."

"You told me about him, Danielle. Yesterday."

"I told you some, but not everything." She looked in his eyes. Even though she trusted him, it was hard to dredge up the past again.

Would he think less of her?

Wayne walked to the chair next to her and sat down. He grabbed her hand. "Young lady, I want to hear all of it. The more I know, the better I can help you."

"I want to tell you everything."

When she finished retelling what had happened at Pauline's house, Wayne put his arm around her. "You are extremely strong, Danielle. I've known it ever since I met you. And now I know why. How many twelve-year-old girls would've had the daring, the courage, the guts to do what you did?"

Hearing him talk about her with such pride made her feel so good. "Thank you."

"Thank you for sharing this with me. What you've told me will help Austin and I to figure out what to do next with the cartel."

"Where is Miguel?"

"We're not sure, but the last report from Austin had the bastard in Texas three days ago. It might be time to get you out of town, Danielle. Those two have a jet. I bet they have a place they could take you to until things settle down."

"That's asking too much of them. I wouldn't dare. They've already gone overboard. Besides, I'm not going to let the cartel or Miguel dictate to me where I can or can't be. I love Wilde. This is my home now." It felt good to say it out loud, to feel it in her very soul. "I'm not leaving."

Sheriff Champion smiled. "Like I said before. You've got courage. I don't agree, but I understand. Just be careful. We will get through this together."

"Yes, we will." *With Lance and Chuck by my side, I can face anything.*

* * * *

Chuck looked at the text from Michael. He and Harry were

coming back early. Once they'd learned about the car incident with Danielle, they'd wrapped up their business at Lake Tahoe fast. He would be glad to have the two back in Wilde. With all that was going on with Danielle, he wanted good friends by his side.

He and Lance grabbed a cup of coffee and asked Carlotta to sit down with them in the booth by the window.

"As you already know, we are Danielle's bodyguards until all of this is settled." Chuck looked into the dear lady's eyes and saw such compassion and concern for Danielle. "We've talked to Sheriff Champion. She is with him now. The sheriff, Lance, and I think it's not safe for her to work after that car incident."

"I agree vith you, completely." Carlotta had such a big heart. "I love dhat girl very much. She is like a daughter to me."

"We care for her, too." The change in Lance was evident.

The truth was both he and Lance had been transformed completely since meeting Danielle. She was the reason for the about-face in their lives. What was once gray was now full of color. What was dull was now full of excitement. He hadn't laughed so much with anyone in years. He was even pondering what it would be like to be with her after everything with Soto and the cartel came to an end.

He couldn't imagine Danielle not being in his life—not being with her. Even now, he missed Danielle, though he and Lance had only left her ten minutes ago at the sheriff's office.

"I see in both your eyes something very interesting." Carlotta tapped on the counter. "I must read you both. And Danielle. Da spirits are restless. I can feel dhey have messages for da dhree of you. I vill come over to Danielle's tonight. I vill bring my cards and my crystal ball. Dis is not up for negotiation, gentlemen."

"We wouldn't dream of trying to stop you." Lance leaned forward. "Actually, I'm a big believer in the spirits."

"I know, but Chuck is not. Correct?"

"That's true," Chuck admitted. "But if anyone could convince me otherwise, Carlotta, I am sure it would be you."

She laughed. "You are right about dhat, Mr. Covington. Vhich one of you vill take Danielle's shift today?"

"That will be me," Lance said.

Austin walked into the diner, his face darkening. The man had a presence that filled any room he entered. "What are you two doing here? Where is Danielle?"

"She's vith Sheriff Champion, Mr. Vilde. She is safe."

Austin looked at them. "Did anything happen at her house last night?"

"That's none of your business," Chuck shot back, angry at the man's audacity.

"I'm simply asking about her safety, buddy. She's okay, right? You didn't see anyone around her place?"

"She's fine, Austin." Lance's hard-nosed timbre spoke volumes. "We walked the perimeter of her house several times and saw nothing."

"Good to know." Austin stood by their booth. "I just got word the cartel killed a guy named Soliz. He's one of their own. Apparently, they believe he stole the four hundred thousand dollars."

Lance sighed. "You mean this might all be over? Danielle will be okay?"

"Maybe. Does Danielle know this Soliz character?"

Chuck didn't like Austin's tone. "Why would you think that?"

"She's keeping secrets. I can tell. Though she didn't say, it was clear to me she knew Soto when I told the sheriff about him."

"She has nothing to do with this, Austin." Chuck felt acid in the back of his throat. He knew Danielle's truth and the horrible past she'd suffered at her stepfather's hands. "Yes, she knows Soto, but she would never be involved in some kind of scheme with him. I am sure she has never met Soliz."

Austin nodded. "I believe you. Hopefully, the cartel doesn't think she was working with their man Soliz."

Chuck jumped to his feet. "Fuck, we've got to go. Who the hell knows when they might try something?"

Lance stepped next to him. There was no other man Chuck would want by his side more than him. "We shouldn't have left her in the first place."

Austin moved beside them. "I understand how you feel. Our sheriff is the best. He won't let anything happen to Danielle."

"Just go. Both of you." Carlotta's gaze remained on Lance and Chuck. "I'm giving you da day off. Da diner vill be fine."

"I'm going, too," Austin said. "I need to talk to the sheriff about this."

With his heart thudding in his chest, Chuck ran out the door with Lance and Austin.

He had to get to Danielle, had to make sure she was safe.

* * * *

"Pauline was from Wilde." Danielle's heartache for losing the woman still stung. "That's why I came here."

"How old was she when you ran away?"

"Seventy-seven." *She would've been eighty-seven if Miguel hadn't killed her.* "Does any of this help you?"

"The more information I get, the better. I'm sure I'll find the murder in the database." Sheriff Champion wrote the information on his notepad. "Do you know her birthday?"

"It was in June, but I don't remember the date."

"That's helpful. It will narrow it down. How old was she when she left Wilde?"

"Sixteen, I believe. I wish I knew her maiden name, but she never told it to me."

"This is more than I had." The sheriff's phone rang. "I'll run this through the database and see what we find on Soto." He picked up the receiver. "Sheriff Champion."

Danielle saw his eyes narrow. He wrote something on his notepad and showed it to her.

There's been a break-in at your house. Maude was shot. Assailant escaped.

Her eyes widened in disbelief.

"Danielle is with me. We're headed that way now." He hung up the phone. "Danielle, do you have your cell?" he asked, standing.

She nodded.

"Call Lance and Chuck and have them meet us at your house."

Before she even brought the phone out of her purse, Lance and Chuck rushed in, the two men she wanted with her more than anyone else, along with Austin Wilde.

Sheriff Champion came around his desk. "I guess you already heard."

Lance nodded. "The cartel is sending a man to Danielle's house."

"Not sending. Sent." The sheriff put his gun belt around his waist. "The thug has already been there and shot Maude Strong."

Chuck pulled her in tight to him. "Let's go."

They rushed out the door.

Lance grabbed her hand. "You okay?"

"I'm fine, but I want to get to Maude as fast as I can."

Chapter Ten

Danielle sat between Lance and Chuck in the back of the patrol car. Austin sat up front with the sheriff, who was driving.

The sheriff turned right onto her street. Her home was ten houses down and on the left.

Austin had told her and the sheriff about the death of Soliz, the man who likely had stolen the four hundred thousand dollars from the cartel.

"Why would they send someone to my house, then?" Danielle's heart was thudding hard in her chest. She prayed Maude was okay. "It doesn't make any sense."

"That's the question I want answered," Austin said. "They may believe you were in on it."

The sheriff parked the car in front. She saw Alex's vehicle and Justin's truck. Maude's car was in the driveway.

They all ran to the front door, which was ajar.

Inside her house was Maude, who was sitting in a chair in her kitchen. Alex was dressing her right arm. Justin, wearing gloves, was checking out the back door.

She rushed to Maude's side. "Are you okay?"

"I'm fine, Danielle. You should see the other guy, though. He fired first. Knocked me to the ground, but I got off a shot before he ran away. Hit him in the shoulder."

"Is she really okay, Alex?"

"She is. Maude is tough as nails. This is only a flesh wound."

"Dad, looks like the guy picked the lock," Justin said.

"Dust it for prints, son. I need to get a statement from you, Maude.

You up to it?"

"Wayne, you heard the doc. I'm tough. I want to get this guy as much as anyone. I came over to fix Danielle's leaky faucet. When I parked my car and saw a motorcycle on the side of the house, I knew something was not right. I wrote down the plate's number. It's in my purse. I also pulled out my gun."

"Mom, are you okay?" Seth Strong ran in with Charly and Heath.

"I'm fine, son. Just giving my statement to the sheriff. Hold on and let me finish."

Charly knelt in front of Maude and grabbed her hand. "Oh my God. What happened to your arm?"

"I was shot, but this old broad is still hunky-dory. Don't worry. Doc will fix me up good as new. Let me finish with my story, okay." Maude turned back to the sheriff. "Like I was saying. I saw the motorcycle and knew something was up. So, I pulled out my—"

"Where's my wife?" Greg Strong ran in with Grant, Maude's other husband, behind him.

"I'm right here."

The two men rushed to her side.

Grant touched her cheek. "Baby, we just heard."

"Are you okay, sweetheart?" Greg placed his hand on her shoulder.

"Yes, honey. I'm perfectly fine. The guy only grazed me."

"Thank God." Grant kissed her.

Both Maude's husbands were tough as nails, but Danielle could tell they were shaken by what had happened to their wife.

Greg stroked her hair. "This was too close, sweetheart. Did you wait for the sheriff? No, of course you didn't. No more taking chances like this one. Understand?"

She winked. "Okay, honey. Let me finish giving the sheriff my statement, please."

"Go ahead," Greg said.

"Where was I? I pulled out my gun and walked to the door."

"I knew it," Greg stated, kissing her cheek. "I'm not letting you out of my sight anymore."

Maude shook her head. "Who is going to run the ranch if you are with me at the hotel?"

"Grant and I can take turns. One of us needs to keep an eye on you, it seems."

Danielle loved seeing how caring Maude's men were with her. Before Maude could continue with her story, in ran the rest of the Strong family, her other sons and Charly's other husbands—Tobias, Nate, Dax, and Drake.

Maude's entire family was by her side, surrounding her with love and concern.

Danielle had never felt that kind of selfless love from her own family. Lance put his arm around Danielle's shoulder and Chuck squeezed her hand.

"You won't be staying here tonight," Lance said. "It's not safe."

"We're taking you to Michael's place. Gather up what you want and we'll get you settled in."

She'd been on her own for so long, her whole life...until they walked into the diner the other day. Ever since, she felt like someone gave a damn about her, someone cared for her. Lance and Chuck were taking hold of her heart.

"Okay, let me finish." Maude was clearly determined to get her story out. "Please. Danielle's safety depends on me telling the sheriff everything."

It wasn't just Lance and Chuck who cared for her. It was Maude. The sheriff. Carlotta. *I must call her as soon as possible.* The whole town. No wonder Pauline had loved Wilde so much. It was the greatest place in the world. It was home to Danielle now.

Maude continued giving her statement. "Average height. I'd guess him to be five-ten or eleven. Lean build. Tattoos on his arms and neck. Dark hair. Dark eyes. Mexican. Late forties. He wore jeans and a blue T-shirt with a Harley-Davidson logo. Leather boots. I heard him drive off on the motorcycle. I saw it when I came up to the house. So as I told you before, I knew something was up, so I wrote down the plate's number. The bike was painted with flames." Maude pointed to her gun on the table. "Be sure to add that he was hit in the shoulder. The left side."

"No one gives that good of a description, much less after being shot." The sheriff smiled. "Maude, you are amazing."

"Yes, she is." After hearing Maude's description of her attacker, an image of Miguel Soto floated in Danielle's mind. "That sounds a lot like my stepfather, Sheriff."

"I've only seen his arrest record photo, but yes, it does." Sheriff Champion got out his phone. "I'll call the state authorities with this description. Justin, you call around to the surrounding clinics and hospitals and see if the guy has showed up at their facilities."

"The cartel has their own doctors on their payroll." Austin, a man who was normally hard to read, was obviously frustrated. "I doubt we'll find him at some public place."

"That's if he can make it to them." Sheriff Champion sounded determined to keep her and the rest of the citizens of the county safe. "Maude is an excellent shot. I doubt the bastard will get far. Austin, talk to your contacts. We need a name. I want to get this guy before he slips back into the cartel's hole. Danielle, is anything missing? The place looks undisturbed. I think Maude must've arrived right after the man broke in."

"Nothing looks out of place here. Let me check the living room." She walked over to the coffee table and picked up the book Pauline gave her. "Same here. Maude saved the day." She walked back into the kitchen and stood in front of the fearless woman. "Thank you. I am so glad you are okay."

"I am, young lady, but I still need to fix your faucet."

She laughed. "It can wait."

* * * *

Miguel's shoulder burned like lava. The bullet that bitch had fired at him had gone clean through. The female doctor had cleaned up his wound. After she'd left his room, he'd slipped out before anyone saw him.

That fucking bitch back in Wilde kept me from getting my book, but it's mine. I won't stop until it's back in my hands, even if I have to kill a dozen people.

Miguel hadn't had a chance to check out Danielle's house for the treasure, only having made it into the kitchen. He had no clue who the woman was. She definitely wasn't Danielle. But he'd fired a shot into her. He hoped it hurt like hell.

Miguel jumped on his motorcycle. He'd stashed his ace-in-the-hole that Soliz had brought him in an abandoned cabin a few miles from town. *Poor Soliz.* The guy was dead now.

Miguel would bring Merle back to Danielle's place. That way, his fucking stepdaughter would be forced to give him the book. Even though those two hadn't seen each other in years, like before, with them, blood was always thicker than water.

Merle was a weak slut and Danielle was a stupid cunt. He'd been able to control them back then, and he would again one last time. Then he would put the two worthless bitches out of their misery for good.

He smiled and headed down the highway, his plan swirling in his head.

* * * *

Lance walked around the outside of Michael's house, checking every bush, every tree, every dark spot.

Every protective fiber in his body had remained tight and on alert since leaving Danielle's house.

Maude had been shot.

That could've been Danielle if she hadn't been at the sheriff's office.

Danielle was inside Michael's place with Chuck.

Sheriff Champion, Justin, and Austin were headed to Elko. They'd gotten word from Dr. Tara Vines that a man with a gunshot wound had been treated there a little while ago.

Lance held a flashlight in one hand and his gun in the other. The shooting was the second time that someone had tried to hurt Danielle. The image of the car careening toward her played over and over in his mind.

His gut tightened.

I won't let her out of my sight again. Am I falling in love with her?

He bent down, shining a light at one of the many rosebushes.

Danielle was everything to him. He hadn't cared for anyone like he cared for her. No woman had ever moved him like Danielle. She was so brave and kind. Funny and sexy as hell.

The cartel issue would be resolved, even if he had to blow away every last one of the drug dealers himself. He and Chuck had the funds to make sure that happened. They could hire the best mercenaries money could buy if need be.

He'd never wanted to go to war with drug dealers, but for Danielle, he would spend every dime he had and fight the devil himself to make sure she was safe.

Hell, I must be in love with her. In his heart, he knew he was.

* * * *

Chuck checked the locks on the windows of Michael's house one more time. The only thing he wanted was to keep Danielle safe.

She was in the bath that he'd drawn for her.

Lance was at the back door, which was made of glass. Not very secure, but he would make sure to keep an eye on it while they were here. He opened the door.

"Everything looks fine outside."

She was safe for now. "All the windows and doors are secure. Danielle is taking a bath."

"Good. That gives you and I a chance to talk."

"About her, right?" He knew his friend was thinking the same thing he was. She could have been killed that afternoon.

"Damn right about her," Lance said. "We can't let anything happen to her, Chuck. She means too much to me."

"To me, too," he confessed. "She's changed me, Lance. I can't imagine a life without her in it. I love her."

"I love her, too."

He sat down at the table. "How can we protect her, Lance?"

"At first light, we take her to the jet. Let's head to somewhere the cartel can't reach."

"Great idea, buddy." He nodded. "Austin said this Rio Grande group runs in the Southwest. I think we should take Danielle to Paris."

"Absolutely. It will be hard to get her to leave Wilde. I can tell she loves it here."

"Hell, I love it here, too. This place gets under your skin fast. No wonder Michael decided to stay."

"Once the dust settles and this cartel issue is finished, we bring her back."

* * * *

Miguel looked at the bitch who had betrayed him. "How fast did it take you to spread your legs for my cousin?"

Before Merle could answer, he hit her in the face and her eyes began to swell.

"That's for the years you fucked the bastard while I was in prison." He hit her again. "You were just as guilty as me."

Merle had refused to testify on his behalf at his murder trial, which enraged him. *So fucking weak and worthless.*

"Our little girl has a nice home here, doesn't she?" He glanced around the kitchen. "We did a great job raising her, didn't we?"

He slapped Merle across the face again, enjoying the look of panic in her eyes.

Blood colored her lips. "Miguel, do what you want to me, but please, don't hurt Danielle."

Kidnapping her had been easy with Soliz's help. After she'd learned that Danielle was still alive, Merle had crept out of Ricardo's bed and house. Soliz had found her trying to start one of the cartel's cars. His old friend had promised to help her but instead had brought her straight to Miguel. Besides handing over the bitch, Soliz also had given him Danielle's address in Wilde, Nevada.

But now Soliz was dead. The four hundred thousand was back in Ricardo's chickenshit hands. Miguel's chance of overthrowing his cousin seemed distant. He needed money. Now.

"Where the fuck did your daughter put my book?" he screamed at his ex-wife.

The whore sat in the kitchen chair he'd tied her to. "I don't know, Miguel. I swear. I haven't seen her since she ran away. You know that."

He'd emptied every drawer, looked in every closet, turned over every inch of Danielle's house. Nothing.

He looked at Danielle's waitress uniform. The name embroidered on the top was where he needed to go.

Someone at Norma's Diner had to know where the little bitch had slunk off to hide. All he had to do was find out who and follow them to his stepdaughter.

Chapter Eleven

Danielle walked into Michael and Harry's living room. The warm bath Chuck had put her in had helped ease some of the tension in her shoulders, but not all of it. How could water wash away all that had happened?

She found Lance and Chuck sitting with Carlotta.

Her boss wore her white turban. "My dear, come sit vith us."

She moved to the sofa and sat between Lance and Chuck. "I'm sorry about my shift, Carlotta. I hope I didn't leave you in a mess."

"Not at all." Carlotta spread out her blue silk scarf on the coffee table and placed her tarot cards and crystal ball on it. "Da spirits are anxious for me to read all dhree of you togdher. I dhought I vould be using da cards tonight, but the crystal ball says 'no.' I am to use it instead."

Lance grinned. "I'm game."

"Me, too." Chuck was clearly open to whatever Carlotta wanted.

Danielle understood. It was hard to resist the dear woman. "I guess I am, too."

"Hold hands." Carlotta pulled out a red candle and a lighter from her purse. She lit the wick. "Did you know that crystals have been used for scrying for dhousands of years? It takes years of practice, gazing at da reflective surface to see into da spirit vorld." The sweet fortune-teller stared at the ball. "I see Lance's parents. Dhey are still among da living, yes?"

"Yes," Lance answered in a quiet tone of awe.

"Dhey are svimming in a large beautiful pool, enjoying dhemselves."

"They have a pool."

"A pool dhat you gave dhem, yes? Wait. Your fadher is getting out of da pool. He's grabbing his cell. Da spirits tell me he's about to call you."

"Really?" Lance's eyes were wide. His cell rang and they all jumped, except Carlotta of course. He looked at the screen. "It is my dad."

Chuck's jaw dropped. "You're kidding."

"Oh my God." Danielle looked at Carlotta with a new level of respect and belief. She was the real thing.

"Hello, dad. Can I call you back? I'm in a meeting. Sure. Thanks."

"He's getting back into the pool now, Lance." Carlotta looked up from her crystal ball. "I told you da spirits wanted me to come tonight. Chuck, shall I dial in your parents' place?"

"I suppose so, but by the look on Lance's face, I'm sure that won't be a problem for you."

"No problem at all." Carlotta's attention returned to the reflective surface. "They are in bed, enjoying—"

"That's all I need to know, Carlotta." Chuck put his hands over his eyes as if he was able to see what was inside the crystal ball, too. "Let them have their privacy."

Carlotta nodded. "I suppose you're right. What about your parents, Danielle?"

She felt the giant hole inside her that had been there since the day she'd run away. "No. Please don't."

"Da spirits believe I should, but I will honor your vishes. Let's see vhat else is in store for da dhree of you." Carlotta closed her eyes and hummed for a few moments. Then she gazed into the orb once again. "Da spirits show much love in your lives. A bright future, full of happiness and joy. You belong togedher. I see children playing around you."

Danielle couldn't help but smile. "Children?"

"I like what you're seeing, Carlotta." Lance put his arm around

Danielle's shoulder.

Chuck squeezed her leg. "How many, Carlotta?"

"Wait." Carlotta's eyes were filled with worry. "Someone is coming. Someone dangerous." She sighed. "I'm sorry. Da vision is gone."

"Whoever is coming will have to face me and Chuck." Lance patted his gun, which was holstered to his side. "We won't let anything happen to Danielle."

"I know." Carlotta took off her turban. "You are meant for each odher. You vill protect her."

Chuck stood, checking the windows and doors. "Yes, we will protect Danielle."

"I must get back to da diner, children."

"Thank you for coming." She gave the sweet fortune-teller a hug.

Carlotta turned to Lance and Chuck, kissing them both on the cheek. "Good-night."

After she walked out the door, Danielle turned to Lance and Chuck. "That was amazing."

Chuck smiled. "She is a true psychic. I'm a believer from here on out."

"How can any of us not be?" Lance shook his head. "I always suspected there were things invisible and supernatural that couldn't be explained, but now I know it for a fact. My God, that thing with my dad and him calling blew my mind."

"Mine, too." Danielle sat down on the sofa. "My head is swirling with all she told us."

"Mine, too." Lance stepped in front of her. "How about a glass of wine, baby?"

"I would love one."

After Lance brought all of them drinks, he sat down on one side of her and Chuck on the other.

"How often do you talk to your dad, Lance?" What kind of parents did he and Chuck have?

"Almost every day. Dad and mom have always been my biggest cheerleaders." It was evident how much he cared for his parents. "We weren't rich. Dad worked for the water department and mom cleaned houses. We didn't have much but we always had fun."

"Any brothers or sisters?"

"Nope. They had me and realized that another child would fall below the perfection they had right in front of them with their baby boy."

"Perfection, my ass." Chuck laughed. "Ellen and Paul stopped because they didn't want to subject the world to another Lance, that's why."

"You only say that because you are the middle child in the Covington family. Marie and Joe had their hands full with you and your siblings." Lance turned to her. "He's got two older brothers and one older sister and two younger sisters and one younger brother. You know what they say about middle children, Danielle? All true when it comes to Chuck."

She loved how Lance and Chuck teased each other. "What do they say about middle children?"

"Middle children, like Chuck, always talk about feeling invisible."

"Not true, buddy."

"I know." Lance smiled. "You're a great friend."

Chuck grabbed her hand and squeezed. "With my mom and dad, none of us felt invisible. Like Lance's parents, mine are my biggest supporters. If I need anything, I know I can depend on them. They always told me to go after my dreams, saying that with hard work, I could have it all."

"And we did, didn't we?" Lance took her other hand. "You know we have money now, but it wasn't always that way. Chuck and I met in college. We were roommates and became instant friends. He became my brother then and remains so to this very day."

Chuck nodded. "Always. We built a company together. It was hard work but so much fun."

"That's how you two made all your money?"

They both nodded.

"I can't imagine what it's like to be able to not worry about what things cost." She sighed, remembering the past ten years of struggle she'd come through. Paycheck to paycheck was all she'd ever known.

Lance shrugged. "Having money is nice, baby, but it doesn't bring real happiness. It's fun, don't get me wrong, but it's the people in your life that matter the most, not the things you can buy."

"We enjoyed building our business, sweetheart, but then we sold it." Chuck's tone filled her with sadness. "We became billionaires but we lost our way."

"Why don't you start another business? If it made you happy before, I'm sure it would again."

"Not a bad idea, baby, but there's something more important that has captured all our attention at the moment." Lance stroked her hair. "You. Business is fun, but you are the only one that will really make me happy. I don't need Carlotta's crystal ball to know that."

Chuck touched her on the cheek. "Even back in the earlier years at college, we both sensed something was missing in our lives. Now I know that was you, Danielle. You are the one we've been looking for our whole lives."

Danielle believed in Lance and Chuck. She believed Carlotta was right. She belonged with them. She needed to tell them how she felt. She loved them. She knew it from the top of her head to the tips of her toes.

Where to begin?

The front door burst open. Lance and Chuck were on their feet in front of her with their guns drawn.

"Put down your weapons." Michael raised his hands over his head. "I surrender. It's just me and Harry."

Lance holstered his gun. "Glad you're home, buddy."

Chuck nodded. "We can really use your help right now."

"When we heard about everything that has been happening, we

came back home as fast as we could. Is Danielle okay?"

"I'm fine, Michael." She came to her feet and walked over to the sweetest gay couple in town. "Better than fine."

* * * *

Lance held Danielle's hand. She'd gotten Michael and Harry up to speed on all that had happened since they'd been at Lake Tahoe.

"I'm beat." Harry stood. "Good-night, all."

Michael kissed him. "Honey, I'll be up in a few minutes."

Danielle yawned. "I think I'm ready for bed, too."

Lance stood and pulled out her chair for her.

Chuck nodded. "I'll finish my beer and be right in."

"Good. I've got something I want to discuss with you." Michael clearly still had something on his mind. He'd invited him and Chuck to Wilde for some other reason that had been put aside because of all that was happening with Danielle. Chuck would get all the details.

Lance walked into the bedroom with Danielle. Life had never been better. He was happy, really happy, and the reason was standing next to him.

Sheepishly, Danielle looked up at him. "Can I ask you a question?"

God, she is adorable. It was clear to him that she had the heart of a submissive. He couldn't wait to introduce her to the life, but it wasn't time. Not just yet, anyway. "Honey, you can ask me anything."

"I care about you and Chuck the same. You do realize that?"

He touched her cheek. Her face was so soft, so beautiful. "I do, and you know we care about you, too, right?"

She nodded. "But my first time was with you. I know Chuck made love to me right after, but you took my virginity, not him."

"Yes, baby." She'd given him the most precious gift a woman could give a man. He couldn't get over it.

Her lip began to tremble ever so slightly.

He pulled her in close. "What's wrong?"

"I'm not sure. I never dreamed I would like having sex so much, but you two make me want it every time I look at you."

"It's not just sex, baby, it's making love. You've set off desires in us we've never experienced before."

"But how can I let Chuck know he's just as important to me as you?"

"You mean because I was the one you gave your virginity to. Now you're afraid he will think he's a third wheel...or something like that?"

"Sort of. I just want him to realize how much he means to me. But I can't give him my virginity. Do I sound crazy?"

He stroked her hair. "Not at all. What if I told you that you could give him something that would be very special, something that would be another first for you, another kind of virginity?"

"I don't understand."

She was so sweet, so innocent. He loved her with all his heart. "Sit on the bed and let me tell you my idea. Chuck will love it. I promise."

* * * *

Chuck finished his beer. "You were right about this town, Michael. It gets in your blood fast."

"I told you it would. So what do you think about my idea?"

"I never thought about owning a television station before, but it is intriguing, especially with the call letters K-I-N-K."

Michael smiled. "This is Wilde, Chuck. They do things differently around here."

"Yes, they do." Putting down roots here made sense to him. "Let me talk to Lance and Danielle about it."

"Lance...and Danielle?" Michael clearly approved. Always the matchmaker. "I like the sound of that, my friend."

"I do, too, Michael. More than you know."

"Danielle looks happier than I've ever seen her. Have you two said those three words to her yet? If you haven't, isn't it about time?"

He'd never spoken those words to any woman before, but spoken or not, he definitely did love Danielle. "You're one to talk. What about you?"

"I've told Harry I love him. I'm not a coward."

Time to turn the tables on his friend. He grinned. "But have you made an honest man out of him yet? Have you asked him to marry you? It's legal in several states, and is recognized by the federal government now. What's holding you up?"

Michael laughed. "Going for the jugular, are you?"

"Hard to give up that playboy lifestyle, isn't it?"

"Not really, Chuck. It's the past. I want to build a life with Harry. Just hoping to find the right time to ask him."

He cared for Michael like a brother. Everyone who ever met the guy did. Michael was charming as hell. "Back to the business at hand. Are you sure the families who support it will be willing to sell to us?"

"More than willing. I've already told Austin my idea and he's on board. With you two running the television station, it will be such a gift to the town. I better head to bed. I've got a handsome devil waiting on me."

"And I have Danielle waiting for me."

He walked into the bedroom and found Danielle and Lance sitting on the bed, both naked. "I thought you two were tired. What's this all about? As if I didn't know already." He smiled, happy with how much Danielle seemed to enjoy sex.

"I'm not sure you know everything, buddy." Lance held up the bottle of lubricant and a package of condoms.

"Wait a second. I'm not sure she's ready for anal sex yet, are you?"

"Ask her yourself."

She stood and walked right up to him.

"Danielle?"

She looked up at him and put her arms around his neck. "I care about you, Mr. Charles Henry Covington."

"I care about you, too, baby."

She tilted her head up, offering her lips. He devoured them, relishing the taste of her. His cock stirred in his jeans.

"I want you to know how much you mean to me." Her sweet gaze unhinged him. "Lance explained some things to me. About the lifestyle you and he are into."

"He did?" He glanced at Lance, giving him his most disapproving look. How could he have thought she was ready for D/s play? She wasn't. Not yet. Sure, she seemed to have a submissive streak deep inside her, but she was so new to sex.

"Not much, but a little."

"Honey, you're not ready for that. Not tonight. There's much more to talk about and go over before we introduce you to BDSM. Trust me, I want that more than you know, but it's not time. I'll know when you are ready." It wouldn't be fair to rush into the life without more time together.

"You're right, buddy. She's not ready for BDSM." Lance gave him that rare look he knew not to discount. It was serious and thoughtful. "But hear her out. I think you'll be surprised what has been going on in this little doll's head."

"What's he talking about, sweetheart?"

"You're just as special to me as Lance. You know that, right?"

"I do."

"I gave him something that I can only give once. My virginity. Yes, you made love to me right after, and it meant the world to me. But I want to give you something that is special, too. Something that you and I can share that will be a first for us."

Realization was dawning on him. "You want me to be your first for anal sex?"

"Yes, Chuck. More than anything. Will you be my first?"

"Hell yes, baby." He lifted her into his arms. "Where have you been all my life, angel?"

"I didn't know it, honey," she said, "but I was looking for you and Lance. Now, I've found you both."

"And we found you." He kissed her, devouring her lips and sending his tongue into her sweet mouth. He placed her gorgeous body on the bed next to Lance. "It's clear that you two will be trouble whenever you are out of my sight." He grinned and began undressing.

"That'll teach you to leave us alone." Her sauciness was just one of the things he adored about her. "Who knows what else we will cook up if you do?"

Lance smiled. "You gotta like how she thinks, buddy."

"Oh, I do." He crawled onto the bed, positioning her between him and Lance. "Come here, you little conniving vixen."

She rolled on her side, facing him. "Like this?"

"Exactly like that." He cupped Danielle's chin. "I want every ounce of your one-hundred-and-nine-pound, sensual body tonight." He caressed her breasts, which were the most perfect pair he'd ever seen or touched in his life. Everything about Danielle was flawless. "Face Lance for me, baby. I want to get your pretty little ass ready for me."

She nodded, and he helped her onto her other side.

"Don't hold back anything, sweetheart."

"I won't. I'm yours." Her words went straight to his need, enflaming it even more.

Lance moved his hand down her body.

Chuck loved seeing her sweet shiver.

"Buddy, she's nice and wet for us."

Chuck nodded and applied lubricant to her soft virgin ass.

Lance began sucking on her nipples, and her breaths turned to pants.

Knowing he needed to take extra time and care with Danielle, since this would be her first time with anal sex, he gently massaged her anus.

After a few minutes, she began to moan. Starting to put a finger into her bottom, Chuck felt her tense.

"It's okay, baby." He couldn't get over how sweet and innocent she was. "I won't hurt you. Trust me. You will enjoy what I have in store for you."

"I will?"

He kissed the back of her neck. "Yes, you will."

"I trust you both."

It thrilled him to hear her say those words. The strength that resided inside her amazed him. She'd survived so much, and now she was his—his to pleasure, to protect, and to love.

"Don't stop breathing." He sent a single digit into her ass, pressing forward only when he could sense her relaxing. Slowly, he claimed a fraction of an inch at a time. Finally, when he heard her moan, he slipped his finger the rest of the way into her hot body.

She gasped.

"Breathe, baby. Breathe."

She nodded and began pushing back into his hand, letting him know she was ready for his cock, and he was ready to claim her ass.

He parted her cheeks and shifted his hips until the tip of his dick was touching her anus. "Ready, baby?"

"Uh-huh," she answered meekly.

"Take a really deep breath for me and hold it."

She obeyed, which only added to his overwhelming desire for her. *She's perfection, through and through.*

"Now, let it out nice and slow."

Again, she complied instantly.

When he knew she was about out of breath, he slowly pushed his cock just inside her virgin depths.

She gasped, and he felt her ass tighten like a vise around his shaft.

"Easy, baby. Keep breathing."

"Like this," she panted.

"Yes. Slow and easy. Very good. How do you feel?"

"I feel wonderful. I feel great." She shifted back into him, taking in a fraction of an inch more of his cock.

"I think she's telling the truth, buddy." Lance had a keen sense about people and clearly could read Danielle like an open book.

"Ready for more, sweetheart?"

"I am," she confessed.

He sent his cock all the way into her beautiful body. *She's mine. This moment is her first time for anal. What a gift she's given me.*

Lance began licking her pussy, and she began writhing like mad.

Chuck's lust was off the leash, and he thrust into her willing body again and again. He grabbed on to her sides and continued his plunges, enjoying the feel of taking her this way.

In and out. Again and again.

He could tell she was getting close from Lance's oral play and his anal assault.

He whispered in her ear. "Come for me, sweetheart. Let me feel you tighten your perfect, soft body around my cock."

"Oh God. Yes. Yes. Yes. " Hearing her screams of ecstasy was all a man could ask for. She embodied absolute feminine perfection.

He, too, was close. Two more strokes into her ass and he came like he'd never come before.

This was more than just sex. This was about Danielle and her gift to him. This was about the connection he felt with her. It was deep.

He could never let her go. Not now. Not ever.

Chapter Twelve

Danielle kissed Lance, who was awake. She could hear Chuck breathing softly, letting her know he, on the other hand, was still asleep. The sun was just peeking over the horizon.

Lance's loving gaze on her gave her a sweet tingle in her belly. "What are you thinking about, sweetheart?"

"Elephants," she answered with a giggle.

His eyes widened. "Elephants? Why elephants?"

"It was a dream I had the night I met you and Chuck."

"Meeting us made you dream about elephants? I don't get the connection."

She told him about the documentary and about the erotic dream she'd had.

He laughed. "Now I understand. I like Africa. Have you ever been?"

She shook her head.

"I think Chuck and I will have to take you there. There's nothing like a photo safari."

"I would love that, Lance. You know what else I love?"

"What?"

"Sex," she confessed, grinning. "Sex with you."

"And with me." Chuck kissed her shoulder. "I hope."

"You're awake. Yes. I love sex with both of you."

"Is it just sex? Are we just your boy toys?" Lance teased.

"You are definitely not boys. You are men." And what men they were. Her heart swelled just being between them. "But no, it's not just sex."

"For me either, baby." Lance's face seemed to glow with happiness. "I came to Wilde for what I thought was going to be another crazy party hosted by Michael, but what I found was you, the woman I want to spend the rest of my life with. This isn't just a passing fling for me. I love you, Danielle."

She offered her lips to him, which he took greedily. She felt tingly all over. "I love you, too."

Chuck stroked her hair. "Sweetheart, I'm a different man than I was when I arrived. You changed me. Everything up to this point in my life was leading me to you. I never believed in magic before, but now, with you, I do. I want you. Nothing compares to you. I love you."

Her heart was his and Lance's, now and forever. "I love you, Chuck." She kissed him and he wrapped his arms around her.

Back and forth, she continued kissing her men until her lips throbbed. She couldn't get enough of them. She finally had a real family. She finally felt loved.

"I love you, Danielle," Lance said, once again.

Chuck grabbed her hand. "I love you very much, baby."

No matter how many times they told her, she would never tire of hearing those words from them.

"I love you both. With all my heart." She kissed them and scooted off the bed. "My turn to make the coffee. You've spoiled me. It's my turn to spoil you." She slipped off the bed and grabbed a robe.

"I wonder if Michael and Harry are awake," Lance said. "If not, you wouldn't need the robe."

She placed her hands on her hips. "Lance Archer, you're a bad boy."

"Wait a second, baby. You just told me and Chuck we weren't boys, but were men. Which is it?"

"Both."

"You've got a body that should be on display. It's beautiful. I'm sure the two gay guys would appreciate it, too."

Chuck nodded. "But not as much as we do, buddy."

"They better not." Lance grinned. "I wouldn't mind showing you off, but only me and Chuck will touch you. That's a hard line for me."

"Me, too," Chuck said firmly.

She saluted. "That's why I'm wearing the robe, Sirs. You never know. Michael and Harry might be closet straights."

They all laughed.

"Stay inside," Lance demanded, which excited her in the oddest way. "I checked the perimeter of the house about an hour ago. All the doors and windows are secure. The alarm is back on."

"Yes, Sir."

She headed into the kitchen and found Harry reading the paper. "You're up early. Where's Michael?"

"In the shower. Coffee is made. Are your guys awake?"

Your guys. She liked the sound of that. "Yes, but I want to bring them their coffee in bed."

"Good girl. Keep your men happy." Harry pointed to one of the upper cabinets. "There's a tray in there you can use. Mugs are to the left of the sink. I'm surprised they trust you with coffee. Didn't you spill tea on them the day you met?"

She grinned, recalling the incident. "Things change."

"Like your feelings for them?"

"Yes. What about you and Michael? Will you be tying the knot soon?"

"I love him, but I'm just a mechanic from Elko. He's a billionaire." Harry put down the paper. "What do I have to offer him?"

"Everything, you nut." Michael walked into the kitchen. "You changed my life. I can't imagine a single day without you in it. I told you that you don't have to work on cars anymore."

"Was that a proposal? I'm sorry, mister." Harry grinned. "I guess I missed that."

"Michael, do you want to marry him?" she asked, uncaring how bold that might be. Her heart was still soaring. She'd found love. She wanted the whole world to experience what she was feeling.

"Of course, I do."

She put her hand on his shoulder. "Then ask him the right way. Get on your knee."

"You're right, Danielle." Michael kissed her on the cheek and then stepped in front of Harry.

"You're really going to do this?" Harry's eyes were wide and the smile on his face revealed how happy he was.

"Yes." Michael got down on one knee. He grabbed Harry's hand. "Will you make me the happiest man in the world, Harry? Will you marry me?"

"I will. Yes. Of course." They kissed.

Danielle left the newly engaged couple, carrying the tray of coffee back to *her men.*

* * * *

Peering through binoculars, Miguel crouched in the bushes, staring at the window he'd seen Danielle pass by moments ago.

Late last night, he'd followed the owner of the diner here after overhearing her talk to the cook about his stepdaughter. She was staying in the home of two queers and was being watched by two other men.

Several times since midnight, he'd seen one of the bodyguards the woman had mentioned were protecting Danielle walking around the entire massive home. Miguel had remained far enough away and concealed that the bodyguard hadn't detected him during his surveys of the area.

Counting the one who came outside from time to time, there were four men surrounding Danielle.

I always knew she would be a fucking slut.

Four to one wasn't ideal, but he needed the book.

An idea occurred to him how he could turn the odds in his favor.

* * * *

"Coffee is served, gentlemen." Danielle placed the tray on the mattress.

Lance pulled her into his muscled body. "Who you calling 'gentlemen?'"

Chuck reached over and tugged on her hair. "You know better, or shall we prove to you again what we're capable of?"

"Absolutely, but later." She couldn't contain herself one second longer. "I've got news, and it's wonderful. Michael just proposed to Harry and he accepted. They're going to get married."

Chuck smiled broadly. "That is good news. I'm thinking about settling down myself."

Her heart began to pick up its pace.

Lance kissed her. "Me, too, buddy. White picket fence, nice house, the whole package."

She began to tremble with joy. "Who's the lucky girl?" Before they could answer, her cell rang. "Damn. Now I'll have to wait to find out." She brought her phone to her ear. "Hello."

The voice she heard made her blood turn icy in her veins.

"Hey, little girl. It's your daddy. Don't tip off your fuck buddies or your mother dies, understand?"

"Yes," she choked out, trying to remain calm. Would Miguel actually kill her mother? She wasn't sure but couldn't take the risk. Though her mother had never made a move to save her, Danielle wasn't about to do anything that would endanger her.

"Very good. Listen carefully. Your mother is at your house tied to a chair in your kitchen. You know what I want. I want my book. The one you stole from me."

"Why?" She could see the concern on the faces of Lance and Chuck growing. Even though she was glad they were here, she needed to hear Miguel out first before she told them he was on the other end of the call.

"Like you don't know."

"I don't know anything."

"By now, I was sure you would've had it appraised. Two days before you ran away, I found an appraisal for the book in Pauline's desk. When I saw it in your hands, I thought you'd seen it, too. God, I forgot how stupid of a bitch you could be." His evil tone sent a chill up and down her spine. "It's a first edition and very rare. Back then it was valued over a million dollars. No telling what it is worth today."

She had no clue that Pauline's gift was worth that kind of money. No wonder Miguel wanted it so badly.

"Bring it to your house. Alone. Be here in ten minutes or your mother dies. If you don't do as I say, I will burn your house down with Merle in it."

"No!"

Lance jerked the phone out of her hand. "Who is this?" he demanded. "The line is dead."

"Oh God, he's going to kill my mother. It was Miguel. He has my mother at my house. He wants my book. I gotta go, now. He said ten minutes."

"You're not going anywhere," Chuck stated flatly. "We are."

"I'll call the sheriff." Lance put on his clothes fast. "I'll have him meet us at Danielle's house."

"Michael," Chuck yelled, finishing dressing. "Get in here."

Michael ran in with Harry right behind. "What's going on?"

"We're headed to Danielle's house. Her stepfather is there with her mother. You two stay here with her. Get your guns." Lance meant business. "Take care of our girl."

"Our guns are in a room upstairs. I'll get them." Harry ran to retrieve his and Michael's weapons.

"Take my book." She felt her heart pounding in her chest harder than it had ever done before.

Lance shook his head. "That's your treasure."

"It is, but my mother's life is worth more than this."

"After all she did to you?" Chuck asked.

"Yes." Until now, Danielle hadn't known that about herself. "She's still my mother."

Lance grabbed the novel. "We'll only use it if we have to."

"We'll take care of her, guys," Michael said. "Go."

Lance and Chuck bolted out the door.

Anxious and unable to just sit and wait, Danielle got one of the outfits she'd brought with her out of the closet. "Can you turn around?"

"Sure." Michael's face was more serious than she'd ever remembered seeing it.

Slipping on her clothes, she heard two gunshots. She gasped.

Michael pulled her to his side. "Quiet."

They listened for any other sound, but heard nothing.

"I'm going to check on Harry. You go get in the closet. Text Lance and Chuck. I'll be right back."

Her pulse raced in her veins. She crouched down in the closet, leaving the door open just a crack so she could see out. "Michael, my gun is in my purse. Take it with you."

He nodded, turning to the nightstand.

She sent a text. *911 – Miguel tricked us. Come back. Gunshots.*

She looked up from her cell and saw Michael reaching into her purse just as Miguel appeared at the door.

He fired his gun at Michael, who fell to the ground with a thud.

Oh God. Not again.

She placed her hands over her mouth, praying the monster wouldn't hear her or see her. Through the sliver of the door and its frame, she saw the man she'd feared her entire life. His jeans were covered in blood. Apparently Harry had shot him. *What about Harry?*

Miguel bent down over Michael. "Motherfucker, where is Danielle? You're hiding her. Tell me where she is."

"Never," Michael choked out, holding his shoulder.

"Too bad, asshole." The bastard placed the barrel of his gun to Michael's head.

The image of Miguel standing over Pauline with the lamp all those years ago burned fresh in her mind. She couldn't let Michael suffer for her mistake. *Time to stop running.*

"Stop!" She opened the door. "I'm here."

Miguel twisted around and faced her. "Just like your fucking mother. A goddamn bitch."

"Take what you want and get out of my house." Michael glared at the man. The bullet had hit his shoulder, and she could see the dark stain of blood expanding on his shirt. He needed to see a doctor as soon as possible.

Miguel kicked him in the head. "Shut your fucking mouth, queer. Yes, I heard who you were at the diner. They love you in this town. I don't. One more word and I will put a bullet between your eyes."

"You want that book, Miguel?" She shoved her fear down as best she could. Their lives depended on her keeping her head. "You better back off."

"Where's my fucking book, bitch?"

"Let us go and I will give it to you."

"You're in no position to negotiate, Danielle," Miguel's tone softened. He limped forward one step. The wound Harry had given him in his leg continued to bleed.

"You need a doctor. You're bleeding." *Michael needs one, too, and probably Harry does as well.*

"So?" He pointed to his shoulder. "This gunshot wound that old lady at your house gave me didn't keep me down."

"So you were the guy on the motorcycle. Maude shot you." *Keep him talking, Danielle.*

"Now you're getting it." His lips twisted in a horrible grin. "All fixed up and good as new. You can't keep me down, Danielle. You can't stop me. Haven't you learned anything, or are you as stupid as you were before? Now, you either tell me where the book is or I will start shooting. First in your legs. Then in your arms. If that doesn't get you talking, I will kill this motherfucker on the floor. I can make this easy or I can make this hard. The choice is yours."

Out of the corner of her eye she saw Michael slowly reaching for her purse, which had fallen to the floor. *He's going for the gun.* "Okay. I'll tell you, but you need to calm down."

"I'm very calm. On the count of three," the creep said. "One."

Michael's fingers were touching the clasp of her purse.

"It's in the kitchen," she blurted out, hoping to buy time.

"You never were a very good liar. Two."

Her heart jumped up in her throat. "Wait. Don't do this. Please. It's at my house. You told me to take it there."

Miguel glared at her. "I told *you* to take it there. Who has it?"

"Lance and Chuck," she confessed, seeing Michael's hand go into her purse.

Miguel stepped to the side and stomped on Michael's wrist. She heard bones cracking.

Michael groaned in pain.

"Good try, amigo." Miguel kept his foot on Michael's wrist, but turned his attention back to her.

Miguel was no longer between her and the door. She wanted to run to it, but knew he would shoot her before she could make her escape for help.

"Now I don't need you anymore. Your fuck buddies have my book. A delay, but I will get it. Time to rid the world of a worthless piece of shit. Good-bye, daughter." He aimed his gun at her head.

I'm going to die and he's going to hunt down Lance and Chuck. I'm so sorry, my loves.

Miguel's eyes narrowed. "Three."

Suddenly, Lance and Chuck appeared in the doorway, their weapons drawn.

Miguel saw them, too, and aimed his pistol their direction.

She screamed.

Before Miguel got off a shot, Lance and Chuck fired their guns, hitting the bastard in the chest and gut.

Miguel's eyes widened and his lips parted just before he crashed to the floor.

Chapter Thirteen

Lance checked Miguel's pulse. The fucker who had tried to kill Danielle was dead.

She bent down next to Michael. "Call for an ambulance. He's been shot."

"Check on Harry," Michael choked out. "We heard shots before that fucker came in here."

His face was pale. He'd lost a lot of blood.

"I'll look for Harry." Chuck ran out the door.

Lance brought out his cell. "You okay, baby?"

She nodded, pressing her hand on Michael's wound, trying to stop the bleeding.

Lance's heart still thudded in his chest. He'd almost lost her, the woman who he wanted to spend the rest of his life with, the woman he loved with all his heart.

"We need an ambulance at Michael Chamberlain's home." He told the dispatcher what had happened, and she promised aide would be there shortly.

"Did you find my mother, Lance?"

"We got your text before we made it to your house. We got a message off to Sheriff Champion. The sheriff, Justin, and Austin were headed to your place to see if your mother was there. Your book is safe and still with us." Lance had left it on the table in the foyer. He picked up his phone again and called the sheriff.

"Sheriff Champion here."

"It's Lance."

"Austin and I are on our way. Just got word from dispatch about the shooting," the sheriff said. "ETA is five minutes. Was it Soto?"

"Yes. He's dead. What about Danielle's mother? Did you get a chance to go inside?"

"The lights were off, so Justin went around back to check things out. I was about to knock on the door when I got the call about what had happened at Michael's. I just spoke with Justin before you called. He's going to check inside. I should hear from him shortly."

"I found Harry," Chuck yelled from upstairs. "He's awake and breathing. The bastard got him in the chest."

Michael closed his eyes. "Oh my God. I've got to go to him."

"You're not moving, buddy." He knew the best course of action was to keep Michael right where he was. "Not until the EMTs get here. Chuck will make sure Harry is taken care of until then."

"Damn it, Lance. I love him. No one is stopping me. Not even you."

Lance looked at Danielle. He understood why Michael was demanding to go to Harry. "Okay. Let me help you, though."

"His wrist is broken, Lance." Danielle was still a little shaken, but he could see her strength shining in her eyes. She was a survivor, after all. "He also might have a concussion. Miguel kicked him in the head."

Michael sat up, clenching his teeth.

The guy was a tough son of a bitch. He helped his friend to his feet, and they all went up the stairs together. Danielle took one side and he took the other. Michael grimaced against the pain.

"Where are you, Chuck?" Danielle called out.

"The master bedroom."

"The second door on the left," Michael whispered.

"Lean against me, buddy. I got you."

As they walked into the bedroom, sirens could be heard approaching.

Harry looked up, his eyes revealing the pain he was experiencing. Chuck compressed the wound in his chest.

Lance and Danielle helped Michael to his fiancé's side.

"I'm here, sweetheart." Michael grabbed Harry's hand. "I'm here."

Lance put his arm around Danielle, who was trembling. "Honey, you and I will go downstairs and wait for the EMTs to arrive." He wanted to get her away from this scene to allow her a moment to catch her breath.

She nodded and they headed downstairs.

He opened the front door and saw the ambulance and the sheriff's patrol car pull up in the driveway.

"Michael and Harry took bullets for me."

"They are heroes in my eyes, baby."

"Yes, and so are you and Chuck in mine."

They told the EMTs where Harry and Michael were just as Austin ran in.

"Danielle, I just got word from Justin," the sheriff said. "He found your mother. She's alive."

* * * *

Holding the book Pauline had given her, Danielle stared at the door with the big red sign that read "Surgery-Hospital Staff Only." Chuck and Lance sat on either side of her in the waiting room.

They weren't alone. Michael's injury wasn't life threatening, but Harry's was. The room was packed with people concerned for Harry.

Carlotta and Deuce had come to give their support. Mackenzie and her two husbands, Wyatt and Wade, walked in carrying coffee for everyone.

Austin held his eight-month-old daughter, Carol, who was asleep in his arms. His four brothers sat around the room, too.

The Wilde brothers' wife, Jessie, was in Michael's room. No wonder, since Jessie had known him since they were children. Although Michael had been sedated, the medication wasn't working well. The nurse had told them that his anxiety about Harry was impeding the shot from working fully. Jessie had decided to remain with him until Dr. Champion came out of surgery with news.

"Quite a crowd," Lance said.

"That's why I love this place." Wilde had taken her in. She'd been nothing more than a castaway, a lost soul. This was her town now. "People here genuinely care about one another."

"I'm glad this wing was completed earlier than expected." Charly, whose baby was due to arrive in less than a month, was the driving force behind Wilde getting the new hospital. "The trip to Elko would've been too far and too long."

The Strong brothers, all six of them married to Charly, sat with her.

Sitting next to Brandon, Shelby looked up from the magazine she'd been reading. "Charly, you might consider speeding it up on the maternity wing, too. With our luck, your baby will come late and mine will come early. Our due dates are only three days apart as it is."

"Yeah, I hear our men have a wager on who will deliver first."

"Actually the whole town heard about the bet, and everyone has gotten in on it. The Champions have an advantage," Tobias said. "They've got Alex on their side."

"Justin and I have just as good a chance as our brother does in guessing the exact time our baby will come." Brandon grinned.

Sheriff Champion held his wife's hand. "We're going to be grandparents."

She, Lance, and Chuck had given their statements about the events at Michael's house to him moments ago.

"Alex is going to deliver both babies?" Austin asked.

Both mothers-to-be nodded.

Danielle knew all the small talk was just an attempt to keep everyone's mind from worrying about what was going on in the surgery room. But it wasn't working. They were all concerned about Harry.

Her mind was still whirling from everything that had happened. "Sheriff, is Justin still with my mother?"

"He is. She's giving her statement to him at my office."

"Do you want to go see her?" Chuck asked. "Who knows how long the surgery will last. We could run over there and be back in no time at all."

"No. I'm not leaving until I know Harry is okay."

Alex came through the doors with a smile on his face. "I just left Michael's room where I gave him the good news. The surgery was a success. Harry is doing fine."

Danielle felt tears of happiness well up in her eyes as the entire group cheered.

* * * *

Following Sheriff Champion and his wife, Danielle walked between Lance and Chuck to his office. She was so nervous. She hadn't seen her mother in ten years, and hadn't really thought about her much for quite some time. She had moved on. Now, she was headed straight to the woman she'd run away from, the woman who had deserted her emotionally long before that.

"How are you feeling?" Chuck asked.

"I'm not feeling much." Inside, Danielle felt detached from her own self. *Ten years.* "My mother hasn't been in my life for a very long time."

They walked up the steps, and Danielle steadied her breathing. Had her mother changed? Or was she the same woman who'd allowed Miguel to beat Danielle? The same woman who'd refused to save her when the monster shoved her in that closet. The same woman who had married the man who killed Pauline and had nearly killed her, Michael, and Harry today.

If I don't feel anything, why am I coming to see her then? Because the truth was, she still remembered the woman who had tucked her in at night when her dad was still alive, the woman who had read bedtime stories to her to help her fall asleep. She missed that woman. Would she find the mother she'd once known inside the sheriff's office? That was only a childish dream.

Still, like it or not, Merle was her mother.

Danielle stepped into the sheriff's office and saw Merle sitting in a chair. Her mother's face was bruised, but she was still as beautiful as she'd remembered.

Merle jumped up and rushed to her, tears streaming down her cheeks.

"My baby girl." Her mother sobbed, hugging her.

Danielle didn't know how to react, and she felt her entire body stiffen.

"I'm so sorry, Danielle." Her mother stepped back, wiping her eyes. "I'm so sorry."

"Let's give the ladies a moment, gentlemen," Chuck said softly.

Sheriff Champion nodded. "Let's clear the room."

Danielle wasn't sure she wanted to be left alone with her mother. What would she say to Merle? What did she want to say?

After the door closed, she came face-to-face with the past she'd been running from for so long. The hurt she'd suffered came bubbling to the surface like the lava from a volcano, hot and deadly. "You say you're sorry. Are you sorry for allowing me to be beaten by that madman? Are you sorry for stealing from all those poor people? Are you sorry for the hell you put me through after daddy died? Are you sorry for being the worst mother on the planet? What? What are you sorry for, Merle?"

Her mother sobbed, but it didn't move her. Not one bit.

"I'm sorry, baby. I'm so sorry. I tried to find you. I swear. I never stopped looking. You're my baby girl. I was a horrible mother. You deserve so much better than me."

"Tell me why you let him hit me? Why didn't you leave him and take me out of that hell?"

"He threatened to kill you, Danielle. I tried to leave. Don't you remember? He found me packing a bag. He beat me and broke my arm."

A memory from long ago floated to the surface of her mind. "You wore a cast for a few months. I remember that. Why didn't you try to leave again?" she asked, though the hardness in her heart was beginning to melt.

"I was terrified, baby. I only wanted to keep you safe. I thought if I could make Miguel happy, he would leave you alone. I cringed every time he beat you. In the beginning, I would always attack him. Every time I did, he beat me and would beat you even more. The last time I tried to stop him, he slammed my face into the floor and he told me if I ever tried to stop him again, he would kill us both. I knew he would."

"I had no idea."

"I kept it from you, baby. Your life was hard enough. You were only a child."

The pieces were coming together. Back then, her mother had told her to obey every word Miguel gave her, to keep quiet and out of his way. Until Miguel had hit Pauline over the head with the lamp, she'd known he was cruel but she'd never dreamed he was capable of murder.

"I even talked to the bastard about giving you away. I thought it was the only way to stop him from beating you, though I knew I would die without you."

Danielle let out a long sigh of pain. "I overheard you talking with him about it."

"Oh my God, baby. I didn't know."

"I honestly thought you wanted to give me away, but you were only trying to protect me."

"I lied to him, Danielle. Those words I told him were lies."

She remembered them as if it were yesterday. "I thought you hated me."

Her mother shook her head. "I love you. I've never stopped loving you. Miguel knew I was lying and refused to let you go. Every bruise he gave you crushed my heart, but I remained quiet, praying for a way to escape the monster one day. I had no money, no friends, no family. Miguel made sure it stayed that way. I only had you. Many of Miguel's family members were powerful drug dealers. Still are. Miguel could turn to them whenever he needed. If I ran away with you, they would find us. I couldn't stand up to such evil men by myself. I was alone. I wish I could've been brave like you, Danielle. I never was. Ever. After your daddy died, I went crazy. He was my rock. Without him, I have been lost. I hope you can someday forgive me for all I've done to ruin your life."

"I want you to know that my life isn't ruined." She knew two amazing men who loved her were standing on the other side of the door. "My life is just fine. Everything you told me is opposite of what I believed was true. I need time to process all of this."

"I understand, Danielle."

She was seeing her mom in a different light. Could they rebuild their relationship? Was it even possible after everything that had happened? For the first time in a very long time, Danielle wanted to try. "You say you weren't brave, but I think you're wrong. We were in that hell together."

"When you ran away my heart broke, but I was glad you were free of Miguel. His family tried to find you, but they never did. I prayed every night you would be kept safe because you were only twelve years old when you left."

"Where do we go from here, Mother?"

"I have agreed to be a witness against the Rio Grande cartel. I have many sins to make right, but I want to start living a better life."

"What do you know about the cartel?"

"I was the prisoner of its leader, Miguel's cousin, Ricardo Delgado. After Miguel went to prison, Ricardo came to me and told me he wanted to take care of me because I was family. I was such a fool to believe him. I moved in with Ricardo, and I soon realized my mistake. The bastard used me any way he saw fit. He believed he could control Miguel once he got out of the pen. I knew better."

"No one can trust the cartel. They don't even trust each other."

Her mother nodded. "The other day, Miguel came to Ricardo and mentioned your name in front of me. I had no idea that Ricardo had already found you. I had to see you, so I snuck out. I told no one, but one of the cartel's men caught me and took me to Miguel. I begged him to let me go. When Miguel told me he knew where you were, I asked him to take me to you. That was just one more mistake of mine to add to the pile. After we arrived at your house, he broke in and made me his prisoner. Miguel is dead, but Ricardo is just as evil. Whatever I can do to make sure he goes away for good, I will do. I want to make things right."

"Mother, you need to forgive yourself. Miguel was the monster, not you. He was the one who beat me. He was the one who threatened to kill you and me. He was the one who murdered Pauline."

"What? Pauline isn't dead, Danielle."

Her jaw dropped. "I saw Miguel hit her over the head and she fell to the floor."

"Baby, that did happen but she survived. As Miguel cleaned out the place, I was able to call 911 without him knowing it. When we heard the sirens, he thought you had called the police. We left poor Pauline on the floor and rushed back to our apartment."

"That doesn't mean Pauline survived, mother. Didn't Miguel go to prison for her murder?"

"Not for her murder but for another." Her mother sighed. "Miguel was trying to move up in the cartel and to impress his father, who was a general in the organization. Long after you ran away, Miguel took me to Ruidoso, New Mexico. At a bar, Miguel bumped into a guy who he knew owed the cartel money. Right in front of me and several other witnesses, Miguel shot the man in cold blood. That's why the bastard went to prison. I was shocked that he got out so early, but I shouldn't have been. Miguel's family is known for their bribes to judges and elected officials. I'm sure they got him out early on a technicality."

She wondered what other horrors her mother had suffered because of that fucker. "I had no idea."

"Pauline did survive, Danielle. I called the hospital and lied, saying I was her daughter from out of state and wanted to know her condition. Without Pauline's knowledge, I've kept tabs on her ever since."

Danielle felt tears well up in her eyes. "She's really alive?"

"She lives in Arizona in a retirement community."

"I have to see her, mother."

Chapter Fourteen

In less than an hour, the guys' jet would be landing in Phoenix. The book Pauline had given Danielle was in her lap. She couldn't wait to see the dear lady who had been like a grandmother to her. They'd called the retirement home but Pauline had been sleeping. The staff had assured them they would tell Pauline that visitors were coming.

I hope she remembers me. The woman was the best part of her past. Pauline was family.

Lance and Chuck were making this trip possible, and she loved them all the more for it.

"I can't get over how beautiful your plane is." Danielle loved every inch of it. She let her fingers squeeze the soft leather of the arms of the plush chair she was in. "I sometimes forget how rich you two are."

Sitting next to her, Lance raised one eyebrow. "Is that a problem?"

"Not at all. Rich or poor, I'm yours. Trust me, even if you had turned out to be the vagrants Carlotta thought you were, I would still have chosen to be with you."

He grabbed her hand and squeezed. "Sweetheart, money is great, but you're the one who brought me happiness."

Sitting in another seat facing them, Chuck tossed a football at Lance. "Who knew you could be so sappy? What happened to the playboy jetsetter you used to be?"

"What about you?" He threw it back. "You're the one who has started writing poetry for our girl, not me. Now that's sappy."

Chuck leaned forward and grabbed her hands. "For this one, I'm nothing more than a fool in love and proud of it."

"I love you two very much." She glanced over at her mother, who was fast asleep.

Lance touched Danielle's shoulder. "Your mom is beat."

"No wonder," Chuck chimed in. "Yesterday was hard on all of us."

"Yes, it was on many levels. I realize now that everything my mother did was only her way of trying to protect me. The wall I created in my heart is crumbling, but it is still quite large. Even though it's going to take time to rebuild our relationship, I do want to."

"Honey, this is a perfect time for us to talk to you about the future." Lance's eyes were full of seriousness and warmth. "Of course you know we want you."

She smiled. "And I want to be with you."

"Wilde is your home, which makes it our home, too." Chuck leaned forward, placing his hands on her knees. "There's a house just out of town that we are looking at buying for you."

Lance touched her on the cheek. "For all of us."

"What house?"

Lance smiled. "The old Wilde Mansion."

Danielle remembered how beautiful the place was, though in need of a little updating. Jessie and Charly had taken her to see it once. "Pappy Jack owns that."

Chuck nodded. "We haven't met him in person, but Michael told us that he's one of the sweetest gentlemen you would ever meet."

"Yes, he is."

"Mr. Wilde hasn't lived in it since his wife died." Lance put his arm around her shoulder. "Sounds like they had quite the romance."

The sweet old man was one of her favorite customers. He loved coming into the diner between rush hours, and she loved hearing him talk about the wonderful life he'd had in Wilde. "I've heard lots of stories about Pappy Jack and his brothers and their wife, Carol."

"Michael and Harry told him that we wanted to stay in Wilde with you." Lance stroked her hair. "The old guy told Michael that if we were interested in buying his home, he would be happy to sell it to us. He said it was time it had a family in it again."

"Sounds like Pappy Jack." She couldn't wait to give the man a big hug and an extra slice of pie the next time he came into the diner. "The place is beautiful. It sits on a hill with trees all around it."

Chuck grinned. "Michael told us that Mr. Wilde is quite fond of you, Danielle."

"And I'm fond of him, too."

"We know that you are in the process of tearing the wall down between you and your mother." Lance's tone was gentle and full of understanding. "And we also know she needs protection since she's going to testify against the cartel. So how would you feel if she lived with us for the time being?"

"It's your call, baby." Chuck's sweet gaze gave her such comfort. "The whole town is ready to protect your mother. If you don't feel comfortable with having her under the same roof, then we'll make other arrangements."

She kissed them both. "You guys think of everything. I've never had anyone take care of me before."

Lance stated firmly, "Get used to it, honey."

"You want her to live with us?" Chuck asked.

"I think spending time with my mom will help both of us heal."

"That's the first time you've called her 'Mom,' sweetheart," he said. "I think the wall is coming down faster than you think."

"It feels like it is. I always had those good memories of her before my dad died. I always loved her, but with everything that happened, my heart hardened against those emotions. Sometimes I have a difficult time opening up."

"After all you've been through, no wonder." Chuck's gentle strength gave her courage and hope. It was easy to trust him. "We'll be here for you through all of it. Trust me."

"I do. Sometimes I want to grab her and hug her and tell her I forgive her everything. But it doesn't feel natural. Maybe it's just simply hard letting go."

Lance kissed her. "Honey, one step at a time. For both of you."

* * * *

Holding the book, Danielle knocked on the door of Pauline's room.

"Come in." The sweet woman's voice sounded just as warm as it had all those years ago.

Her mother smiled. "You go, Danielle. Talk to her alone. If she's willing to see me, I'll come in after."

"She's right," Lance said. "Chuck and I will stay in the hallway with your mom."

She nodded and opened the door.

Pauline looked up from the chair she was sitting in. "Danielle, is that you, my sweet child?"

She remembers me!

Tears welled up in her eyes. "Yes, it's me." She ran over and hugged her. "I missed you so much."

Pauline hugged her back. "I missed you, too."

"I brought the book you gave me." She held it up in front of her. "I took it with me everywhere. Whenever I was in trouble or afraid, I would read it and remember all the things you taught me. It made me stronger and gave me courage to get through the dark times. Oh, Pauline, I thought you were dead. Please forgive me for running away."

"You have nothing to be sorry for, young lady." Pauline wiped the tears from her eyes. "You were in a terrible situation. You were a child. You did nothing wrong. I've missed you and prayed for you every day since the attack. Tell me everything that has happened to you, Danielle."

"I live in Wilde because of the stories you told me about when you were a girl."

"Oh my." Pauline's eyes lit up. "That's wonderful. I have a cousin who lives there still. You may have met him. Jackson Wilde is his name."

"Pappy Jack is your cousin? Of course, I've met him."

"I haven't seen him since Carol's funeral. He's the only family I have left."

"That's not true, Pauline."

"I guess not. He has three sons and five grandsons, too."

"That's true, and they are all wonderful men. Your grandsons are married to a very dear friend of mine and they are happy as can be. But I'm not talking about the Wilde clan. I'm talking about me. I'm your family, too—and you are mine."

"I love you, child. I've missed you so much."

Danielle recounted what had happened the day she'd run away and everything that had followed. The sweet lady smiled when she talked about how she'd fallen in love with Lance and Chuck. Pauline listened intently when she told her about how she and her mother had been brought back together by Miguel's death.

"My mother and my guys are right outside. She would like to talk to you, but that is entirely up to you."

"Merle was in a very difficult situation, too, Danielle. You were too young to know, but I could see it every time you, she, and Miguel showed up to my house. I learned that a woman called the ambulance after Miguel attacked me. I have no doubt that was your mother." Pauline sighed. "Yes, I want to talk to your mother, too. Bring her in, child."

Danielle opened the door. "Mother, come in."

Her mother ran through the door and fell to her knees, sobbing. "I'm so sorry, Pauline. Please forgive me."

Pauline stroked her mother's hair. "You saved my life, Merle. Don't you know I could see right through Miguel and the prison he kept you in? I was trying to find a way to pull you and Danielle out of that horror, but before I got a chance to do it, the bastard attacked me. I never saw any of you again. Danielle told me he's dead. Somehow I have to find a way to forgive him for his evil deeds. You did nothing wrong. You were doing your best to protect Danielle."

Pauline could see the silver lining in the darkest of clouds. She was a saint.

Her mother continued to sob and put her head in Pauline's lap. "I missed you so much. You were like a mother to me."

"I know, my dear. Poor thing. Your mother died when you were so young."

Tears rolled down Danielle's cheeks as her giant wall against her mother came crashing down. She bent down and put her arms around her mom and Pauline.

"Mom, I love you."

* * * *

Chuck leaned against the wall in the hallway outside Pauline's room. Lance stood next to him.

Danielle came out of the door, her eyes red and puffy, clearly from crying. The smile on her face told him they'd been happy tears. "Pauline wants to meet you."

Lance put his arm around her. "And we want to meet her, too."

Chuck grabbed her hand. "Lead the way, baby."

They walked into the room together. Danielle's mother sat on the bed facing the elderly woman, whose eyes were full of life and joy.

"These must be the young men you were telling me about, Danielle. They are quite handsome. I can see where the attraction came from. You two will be good to my girl, won't you?"

"Yes, ma'am," he and Lance said in unison.

Pauline's whole face lit up. "Merle, look how happy these three are."

Danielle's mother smiled. "They do seem good together."

"Have a seat, young men." Pauline didn't look like a woman of eighty-seven years, and she definitely didn't act it. "I want to hear all about you and your time in my childhood hometown."

They all talked for a couple of hours. Pauline had some of her own stories that made them all laugh. This felt good. This felt like family. It was clear to him by the way Danielle kept hugging her mother that the walls she'd built up over the years were gone. He was glad. He wanted the love of his life to be happy. She had her mother again and Pauline.

"Would you ladies excuse me and Lance for a moment? I would like to discuss something with him in the hallway."

Pauline smiled. "Just like my Ernest. Go. Have your man talk."

Chuck bent down and kissed the dear woman on the cheek. "Thank you, Pauline."

Lance kissed her on the other cheek. "You've made our girl very happy."

"And I just got a kiss from each of you. You've made my day, young men." She winked. "Leave us ladies to our talk now."

He and Lance nodded and walked out the door.

Lance turned to him. "What's up, buddy?"

"I know we talked about moving Danielle's mother in with us already, but—"

"Get out of my head. You and I are thinking the same thing. We need to move Pauline back to Wilde and in our new home, right?"

"Yes. Exactly."

"You think she'll agree to that?"

"I think we should talk to all three of the ladies first, but I know that's what they need. There is still much catching up to do and healing to come."

"Chuck, that's why you're the brains and I'm the pretty one."

"I'm the brains and the pretty one, Lance," he teased. "You know that."

Chapter Fifteen

Danielle stood in front of the old Wilde Mansion. "I can't believe this is actually our home."

"I'm just glad we finally get to move in." Chuck sighed. They'd all grown anxious over the past few weeks. "I was getting tired of hotel living."

"Don't tell Maude Strong that." Lance had enjoyed the room service at the Hotel Cactus much more than the rest of them. "She is very proud of her new hotel."

"The new Cactus is very nice, but it's not the same as being in your own place." Chuck pulled Danielle in tight, turning to her mom and Pauline. "Don't you ladies agree?"

Her mom nodded. The bruises on the outside had healed, but Danielle knew it would be some time before the bruises on the inside would.

She grabbed her mother's hand and squeezed.

Pauline, who looked ten years younger since they had sprung her from the retirement center, headed up the steps. "I completely agree with you, Charles." Pauline was the only one left that called Chuck by his given name. He seemed to actually like it from her.

Since bringing her back to Wilde, the dear lady had reunited with her cousin, Pappy Jack, and had met the rest of her extended family. She looked more vibrant than ever. Wilde did that to a woman.

"Shall we see inside?" Lance asked.

"Definitely." Danielle went up the stairs to the entrance of the grand home.

I'm going to be living in a mansion. An actual mansion.

They walked through the double doors to the foyer, which had the most beautiful, sweeping staircase she'd ever seen. It could've been featured in Architectural Digest or one of those other home design magazines.

Chuck offered his arm to her mother and Pauline. "Shall I escort you to your rooms, ladies?"

Her mother shook her head. "We've been here during the remodeling, son. Pauline and I can find our way. I think you three should take the tour together. We'll catch up with you later."

Danielle put her arms around her mother. "Thanks, Mom."

"You're welcome, sweetheart." Her mom and Pauline walked hand in hand to the back of the house where their bedrooms were. They even shared a bath and a sitting room. It was good to see how wonderfully they were getting along. Forgiveness did heal deep wounds.

"What do you want to see first, baby?" Chuck always put her needs and wants before his. Loving him and Lance was like breathing now.

She giggled. "Our bedroom, of course."

Lance kissed her. "We thought you might."

"No time like the present." Chuck pressed his lips to hers.

She walked between them up the stairs to their bedroom. "I think we better call this the Masters' bedroom, as in plural, don't you agree? There are two of you."

Chuck grinned. "Not so subtle, baby."

"What do you mean?" She feigned innocence, but knew he was seeing right through her.

"You know exactly what I mean," he said firmly as they walked into the bedroom.

She couldn't believe her eyes, seeing all the roses around the room. It was the most beautiful place she'd ever seen, but the flowers reminded her of their very beginning together. She turned and kissed each of them passionately. "This makes me so happy. I feel so at home now."

Lance pulled her in tight. "We wanted this to be special for you, baby."

"I'm glad you like it." Chuck stroked her hair.

She grinned and placed her hands on her hips. "You're not off the hook yet, guys. I love you, but I believe I told you I like sex. So let's get back to BDSM."

"You're being quite sassy, baby." Chuck's deep tone took on a dominance that she instantly responded to. "We've told you a lot about the life. What happens to a submissive when she's bratty?"

"The problem is that all you do is talk. I think I know more about how things work than a lot of people practicing the lifestyle. I am ready."

Lance smiled. "You think so?"

"Yes."

He cupped her breasts. "Really?" His deepening tone sent a shiver up and down her spine.

She nodded.

"What do you think, Chuck? Is our girl ready for a demonstration?"

"Let me call Austin and see if the room we reserved for tomorrow night is available now."

She grinned, realizing they'd already planned everything for her introduction into BDSM. "You are both devils."

"No. We are your Doms, honey." Chuck kissed her, making her toes curl and her belly flip-flop. "I told you we would know when you were ready to dip your toe in the water of our life. It turns out you're ready to dive in headfirst. Hello, Austin. This is Chuck."

As Chuck made plans for them to go to the club, Lance pinched her nipples, delivering a sting that made her tingle from head to toe with excitement.

"Don't forget who is in charge, sweetheart." Lance's Dom side was coming through loud and clear.

She trembled, remembering all the discussions they'd had about protocols. "I won't forget, Sir."

The smile that spread across his face warmed her insides nicely.

"Come here, sub."

She did, and he led her to the largest closet she'd ever seen, complete with a vanity and full-length mirror. Seeing it on the architect's plans was one thing, but seeing it finished was another. "This is much bigger than the bedroom in my old house."

"And it's all yours, baby. Chuck and I will share the other closet." From one of the shelves he grabbed a gift-wrapped package. He handed it to her. "This is for you."

She opened the box and found a sexy one-piece outfit made of black leather with a zipper that ran from top to bottom in the back. Also inside was a pair of stilettos to match. "You already bought this for me?"

"Yes." He kissed her. "Put it on, now."

Chuck got off the phone. "A day earlier than we planned to take you to the club, but you're a naughty, impatient girl who needs to learn her lesson."

She giggled. "Yes, I am, Sir. Yes, I am."

* * * *

Walking into The Masters' Chambers, Danielle tugged on the too-short skirt that Lance and Chuck had bought for her. The cool air on her exposed skin excited her, but still she was nervous. She knew that anyone could see she wasn't wearing panties—another requirement by her two Doms.

They stood protectively on either side of her as they approached the desk of the reception area.

Austin sat behind the desk. "Everything is ready. All I need is yours and your sub's signatures."

Your sub's...? She liked being called their sub.

They read the paperwork and signed it.

"Here's the key," Austin said. "Room seven."

They walked through the door into the main area of the club. She'd never been there before, but had heard how elaborate it was from Jessie and Charly. A few people were milling around, but it was early. She wondered if later the club would be packed to the rafters.

Lance and Chuck led her down a hallway. They both wore black leather Dom outfits that enhanced their masculinity and muscles perfectly. Her men oozed power and dominance.

When they came to room seven's door, her heart was racing as Chuck put the key in the lock.

This is it. I want this, but I am so nervous.

Wouldn't they be surprised if she blurted out the safe word they'd agreed on now? She giggled. No way was she going to yell out "thorns."

She wanted to experience the lifestyle they enjoyed. She wanted to please them. Taking a deep breath, she gathered her courage. This would be fun. She trusted them. Tonight, she would say only "roses" to let her Doms know she wanted to continue.

Chuck opened the door and his hot gaze landed on her. "Time to find out how you like BDSM, sub. Inside."

She lowered her eyes. "Yes, Sir. Roses. Roses. Roses."

They both laughed.

Chuck shook his head, but she could see the grin on his face. "She's trouble."

"Just the right kind of trouble we love, buddy." Lance put his arm around her.

Stepping into room number seven surprised Danielle. It was bigger than she'd imagined such a room would be. Scary-looking, yet exciting, too.

The walls were a dark gray with shelves and hooks loaded with all kinds of sex toys. To her left was a bench, reminding her a little of a massage table. To her right was a contraption with cuffs for both hands and ankles. In the center of the room was a strange-looking bed with pillars on each corner.

"Sit on this bench," Lance commanded.

"Yes, Sir." She sat down and faced him.

He bent down and removed her stilettos. "God, these are gorgeous." He ran his hands up and down her legs freely, causing her insides to warm. "On your feet," he said, taking a step back.

"Yes, Sir," she answered as she'd been instructed to. She wanted to make them proud, to prove to them she was capable of being a good sub.

Lance and Chuck circled her, each touching her all over. Their lusty gazes went up and down her body again and again.

"Very nice." Lance looked like a hungry predator and she was his prey. "Very nice indeed."

"Sexy as hell, that's for sure." Chuck's words came from deep in his chest, like a growl.

Their sinful smiles and wicked words were getting her hot and excited.

"On your knees, sub. Now." Chuck's tone left her trembling.

"Yes, Master." She'd practiced kneeling with them at home several times. She got down on the floor, knees together, stretching her toes and laying the tops of her feet on the floor. Her bottom rested on the back of her calves.

"Very good." Lance tugged on her hair slightly. "Put your hands behind your back."

She obeyed, remembering to keep her eyes lowered. "Yes, Sir."

His hand released her strands and moved to the back of her neck. "What state are you in, pet?"

"Roses, Sir." She stared at the tops of his and Chuck's leather boots. She loved that they were in charge.

"Where shall we begin with our submissive, Chuck?"

"First, let's unwrap our present." Chuck unzipped her outfit slowly and sensuously. He kissed his way down her naked back with each inch the zipper traveled. He removed the one-piece, leaving her totally exposed.

What happens next? She trusted them with all her heart, but the unknowns around this room and this play made her both anxious and excited.

Lance and Chuck put their hands under her arms and lifted her off the floor. They guided her back to the bench.

"Bend over," Lance demanded.

The dominance in both their tones was getting to her on several levels.

"Yes, Master." She felt a swirling tingle in the center of her belly that spread out through the rest of her body.

They pinched her bottom and fondled her pussy until her breathing became labored. Then she felt one of them apply lubricant to her ass. Which one was going to send their dick into her bottom? She'd never even fantasized about anal sex before, but over the past few weeks with them, she'd come to love the experience and feel of it.

Chuck came around to the other side of the bench and knelt down in front of her. He touched her cheek. "Look me in the eyes, sub."

She obeyed, gazing into his dark orbs.

"We're going to put this in that gorgeous ass." He held up a blue sex toy that was shorter but thicker than her vibrator, which had gone unused since meeting her two men. "Notice how it is flanged at the end, pet. This is for anal play. You're going to love it, I promise. I want you to tighten down on it while it is in your body no matter what happens next. Tight as you can, understand?"

"Yes, Sir. I will try." *What else do they have in store for me?*

He tugged on her hair, causing her to gasp. "Don't try, baby. Do it. Do as I say."

She nodded, chewing on her lower lip as Lance continued stretching out her anus with his thick, slicked-up fingers.

"Good girl." Chuck disappeared from her view, walking to the other side of the bench where her ass was on full display.

He and Lance worked together now, one spreading her cheeks and the other placing the toy at her tight ring.

"Big breath, sub," Chuck ordered.

When he shoved the plug into her ass, she let out all the air she'd just taken into her lungs. The sting lasted only a split second, followed immediately by her pussy dampening and her clit throbbing.

Another order came from Lance. "Roll over on your back."

"Yes, Master." As she did, the toy inside her bottom stretched her more, reminding her to clamp down on it as she'd been instructed.

Facing the ceiling, she saw Lance and Chuck move on opposite sides of the bench. Their hot stares delighted her and made her shiver.

The bench was more versatile than she'd first thought. There were additional parts attached to it that had been tucked under the seat. Lance folded out two arm extensions, and Chuck pulled out two leg extensions. There were clamps on each of them. Her two Doms attached her wrists and ankles to the extensions. She was spread out like the letter *X*.

I'm totally vulnerable to them. Everything inside her was responding to their dominance over her.

Lance held up another toy. It had a metal ring, which had three silver chains hanging from it. At the end of each of the chains was a little clamp with rubber tips. "Do you know what this is?"

"No, Sir."

"This is a Y-clamp, pet." He bent down and licked her nipples, which instantly began to bud. "Two of the clamps are for these beauties. Can you guess where the other clamp goes?"

Her heart thudded in her chest. He couldn't mean down there, could he? "I'm not sure, Master."

He pinched one of her nipples and Chuck pinched the other, delivering two delicious stings.

"I asked you a question and I expect an honest answer, sub."

She whispered, "On my clit. Maybe."

"Maybe is right. On this sweet little nub." He pressed his thumb on her clit, increasing the pressure inside her.

Chuck brought his fingers to the side of her face. "Don't forget to tighten on the plug in your ass, sweetheart."

Instantly, she stiffened around the toy. More moisture dripped from her pussy. She'd never been so wet in all her life.

Lance attached the clamps to her nipples. The compression made her squirm. It felt like sweet jolts that created sparks on every nerve ending inside her.

"Her lips are quivering nicely, Lance." Chuck's unwavering attention added to her excitement. "I think they are adjusted perfectly for her."

They were watching her every move, discerning her every need and discomfort. Knowing how careful they were being with her made her trust them even more, love them even more.

Chuck bent down between her legs and began licking her pussy until she was writhing on the bench, out of control. When he captured her clit with his teeth, she moaned.

He released her and she instantly missed the feel of his mouth on her pussy and clit. "Time to clamp this baby."

"I agree." Lance applied the third part of the toy to her tiny bud of nerves. The bite of the clamp sent a shock through her entire system, and her clit began to ache like mad.

Chuck smiled. "You're doing great, baby. Time for you to experience some dual action."

Isn't that what I've been experiencing already? "Yes, Sir."

Lance held up a vibrator. "You know what this is, I'm sure. I'll be using this on this gorgeous pussy."

A fresh blast of need shot through her.

Chuck held up a long thin device that had a cord and plug attached to it. "This is a violet wand. I'm going to start you on the lowest setting and build up to see how much you can take, understand?"

"Yes, Sir."

"I'll be watching you very closely to push you to your edge but not past it. Your job is to say your safe word when you need to, understand?"

She nodded, realizing how serious he was about this. Unable to move or resist, she wondered what that toy would feel like on her naked skin. Her nipples and clit were throbbing intensely from the clamps. Was she reaching her limits? She didn't think so but wasn't entirely sure. *What is coming next?*

They both smiled, turning on the toys in their hands. The vibrator's hum was at a lower frequency than the wand, though they almost seemed to harmonize with each other.

"Look here," Chuck commanded, holding up the electric toy in front of her.

She saw a warm light shooting up the glass tube. He touched the tip of the wand to her abdomen and she saw the light jump from it to her skin, instantly feeling the spark nipping at her flesh.

Lance brought the vibrator to her swollen, wet folds, its pulse on her pussy sending her into a delirious dizzy state.

Chuck removed the clamps from her nipples, and she could feel her pulse as her breasts began to swell even more. He brought the tip of the wand to each nipple, raising her need and increasing the overwhelming pressure inside her.

Lance removed the clamp from her clit, replacing it with the toy in his hand. The oscillation drove her crazy. Reaching her limits, she needed them inside her. *Both of them.*

The plug in her bottom and the vibrator on her pussy could not satisfy her the way they could. Their total domination of her body— their cocks plunging into her depths, into her very soul—was the only thing that would quench the fire of desire they'd fanned from her.

"Please, Masters. Please. I need you. I need you so badly."

"Our sub is begging so sweetly, Lance." Chuck kissed her on the cheek, tapping the handle of the plug, sending a fresh vibration into her ass. "Has she earned her reward?"

Lance fingered her pussy, making her even wetter. "I believe she has."

Danielle was panting like a crazy woman by the time Chuck removed the plug.

She watched them strip out of their leathers. Even though she'd seen them naked many times over the past few weeks, they still took her breath away.

In a flash, they had her out of the cuffs. Chuck lifted her into his arms. Shivering from head to toe, she wrapped her arms and legs around him.

They all headed for the bed. She kissed Chuck's chest, as he stretched out on the mattress, pulling her on top of him. She could feel his hard cock pressing against her thigh. He shifted his body until the tip of his cock was touching her pussy.

She wiggled her hips, urging him inside, her thirst overpowering.

He thrust into her, filling her with his thick dick, scraping against the spot deep inside her pussy. The pressure rose higher and hotter.

"Oh my God." Feeling him touch that special place again, like the first time she'd made love with him and Lance, sent her into a state of delicious dizziness. She wondered if it could get any better. But it always did.

Lance moved on top of her, pinning her tighter between him and Chuck. The weight of his muscled frame felt so good, so right. He sent his cock into her ass, stretching her and expanding the sensations in her body.

"Oh God," she whimpered. Feeling their dicks inside her increased her maddening need. "Yes. Please. More, Sirs. More."

"Yes, baby." Lance kissed her neck. "I will give you more."

"Mmm. I love you, Master Lance. I love you so much."

Chuck's hot breath sent a fresh shiver through her body. "I want more of you, too, sweetheart."

She panted, wild with desire. "I love you, Master Chuck. God, I love my two Doms."

Lance's voice deepened into a possessive tone. "I love you, baby. Take me deeper until I can feel every inch of you. God, you are so fucking hot."

Hearing his passionate words drove her insane, increasing her want.

"I love you, sweetheart." Chuck's thrusts lengthened inside her pussy. "You are mine. All of you. Giving you mind-blowing pleasure is all I desire." The dominance in his every syllable made her even hotter. "I will never let you go. Understand?"

She opened her mouth to answer him with the appropriate response, but the words wouldn't come out. Her heart was racing as she stammered out something unintelligible.

"That's my girl." He growled his approval, thrilling her.

She wanted this moment to last but wasn't sure how much more she could bear. Her skin was on fire from the burn they were creating in her body.

Lance and Chuck sent their cocks into her depths. In and out. Over and over. Again and again.

Lines of electricity ran up and down her. "I can't take this anymore. Oh God. Too much. But I need...more. Please. Yes." Sizzling inside and out, she pulsated from head to toe, unable to still a single inch of her body.

She fisted the sheets, trying to hold on for dear life.

"She's close, buddy." Lance's words were filled with heat.

"I can sense it, too." Chuck continued invading her pussy with his cock. "Come for us, Danielle. Come now."

Unable to resist their commands, she felt her pussy begin to spasm.

Their synchronized thrusts came faster and deeper, sending her over the edge into the most explosive orgasm she'd ever experienced in her life. It was earth shattering and body shaking. Every inch of her could not be kept still. She vibrated like a live wire, and tears of release welled up in her eyes.

"Ahhh." Lance groaned, reaching release. Her ass clamped on his cock. She could feel it pulsating inside her.

Chuck's eyes narrowed but never closed, never faltered from her. One final thrust into her body, and he came. Her pussy tightened again and again on his dick as he climaxed inside her.

Totally exhausted and unable to move a single muscle, Lance and Chuck rolled her onto her side, between them, raining down kisses all over her skin.

Riding the softening sensations zipping through her body, she felt completely spent, completely satisfied. The lifestyle that Lance and Chuck had shown her was one she wanted to explore more—with them.

This was where she belonged, in the arms of her two Doms.

Chapter Sixteen

Chuck's home, the old Wilde Mansion, teemed with every person who lived in the town.

The crowd included all six of his brothers and sisters, as well as his and Lance's parents. He and Lance had flown them in several days ago and they'd instantly fallen in love with Danielle, and she with them.

Though their families were a little taken aback at first at the idea that they were sharing her, their parents and his siblings had come around after a few bottles of wine and a lot of reminiscing, which had Danielle laughing about their growing-up years. The discussion had turned to the future and how they both loved her and wanted to spend the rest of their lives with her.

Danielle had stood, courageous as always, and had shared her feelings about him and Lance. "I love them."

No sweeter words could be spoken.

Their parents and his siblings gave their blessings, uniting them forever as a family. The one thing that you could always count on in the Archer and Covington households was love, support, and especially understanding.

The band ended their set, pulling Chuck's attention back to the party.

Maude Strong and Mary Wilde, along with their respective husbands, had put the housewarming party together for him, Lance, and Danielle. He couldn't get over how generous and warm Wilde was.

Carlotta sat in a corner of the room, offering free tarot card readings to everyone. Danielle's mother, Merle, sat in the chair opposite her, hearing what her future would be.

He was glad that Danielle and her mom had grown so much closer the past few weeks. Merle was brave, just like her daughter. Her testimony would put some very bad men away for a long time. Keeping Merle safe was one of his and Lance's main priorities. In fact, the sheriff, Austin, and the whole town were making sure to keep an eye out to protect Merle.

He glanced over at Pauline, who was talking with Pappy Jack. The woman had never had children of her own, but she saw Danielle as her granddaughter and Danielle definitely thought of Pauline as her grandmother.

Little Carol crawled around her five dads' feet. Austin and his brothers were terrific fathers. Family meant everything to the people of Wilde. Chuck couldn't wait to start a family here with Danielle and Lance. It would be the greatest place in the world to grow up.

Mackenzie, the wife of Wyatt and Wade Masters, stood beside him and Lance. "This is some housewarming."

"Seems to me that the people of Wilde like any excuse for a party," Lance told Mac.

She'd been promoted to president of their newest venture in Wilde, AC3W Media Group. It was a fledgling company with only two holdings so far, both of which were in Wilde. KINK-TV and the local newspaper, Wonders of Wilde.

Chuck was excited to be a part of AC3W. He and Lance had been on the bench and out of the game for far too long. This was going to be even more fun than when they'd built their first company together.

Michael and Harry came over, carrying drinks and food.

"Here you go." Michael handed Mac a glass of wine and got beers for Lance and himself. "I am glad to see the power team is already getting together. How are our co-CEOs and madam president doing this fine night?"

"You're too much, Michael," Lance said. "Don't you ever stop working?"

"He never does." Harry smiled. "I've been trying to nail him down about some of the wedding plans, but he's so excited about the new company I can't get him to focus."

Michael put his arm around his fiancé, who had fully recovered from the shooting. "Archer-Covington-Chamberlain-Canyon-Wilde Media Group. I'm Chamberlain. You're Canyon. Both our names are on the line, honey."

"We're all in, Michael. You've won." Chuck knew he'd won, too. He had found the love of his life and also a new home, a new town to put down roots and raise a family. "You have me and Lance and Austin all tied up in your scheme to put Wilde on the map."

"Not on the map per se, but at least where likeminded people will be able to find our town. Look at you and Lance." Michael grinned and pointed at Danielle, who was on the sofa talking to Shelby, Jessie, and Charly. "You found true love here. Others will, too, with our help."

"Then why not start a matchmaking company instead of a media group?" Mac teased. "It would be easier, and we already have our Cupid right here."

They all laughed.

"Mac, the article you wrote in yesterday's paper was excellent," Harry said. "You are definitely the right person for the job."

Chuck completely agreed. "Have you learned any more about Ricardo Delgado's whereabouts?"

Mac shook her head. "He's off the radar completely, but I'm talking with a contact I have in Destiny, Colorado. His sources are searching every database, both private and government, for any sign of the creep."

Lance took a drink of his beer. "That's some source."

"Sounds like a CIA guy to me," Michael said. "Or at least someone who has been in the Agency."

"Dylan Strange was in and out and now is back in again, or so I'm told." Mac smiled. "I did find out that he's married now, and you know what that means."

"What?" Harry asked.

"He's even better than before." Mac pointed to her husbands. "Just like my guys."

Lance nodded. "A woman does that for a man."

"That's for sure." Chuck turned his gaze back to Danielle, the love of his life.

"Or a man for a man," Michael added. "Right?"

"Absolutely. Your wedding will be the event of the summer. Everyone in town will be there."

Harry grinned. "We actually have to have two weddings. The legal one is in Tahoma, California, which is right on Lake Tahoe near Michael's vacation home."

"It's not *Michael's* place, Harry. It's *our* place. Everything that is mine is yours. You know that. Too bad Nevada hasn't caught up with the times yet. The real wedding will be here, in Wilde, with our friends and family."

Chuck looked at Lance. "I think that's our cue, buddy."

"Yes, it is."

Chuck cleared his throat. "May I have everyone's attention, please?" As everyone turned to him, the only person in the room that held his was Danielle. God, she was so beautiful. "Come over here, sweetheart."

She smiled, though her eyes questioned what was going on.

He and Lance led her to the stairs, asking her to step up on the first rung. They wanted everyone to see their gorgeous woman.

"What's this about?" she asked.

"On three," Lance said to him, and they both counted in unison. "One. Two. Three."

They both got down on one knee and grabbed one of Danielle's hands.

Her cheeks turned a bright pink and tears welled in her eyes. "Oh my God. This isn't what I think it is, is it?"

"If you think this is something other than a marriage proposal, then you're mistaken, because it is," Lance teased, and then turned serious. "I love you, Danielle. My whole life I've been looking for you even when I didn't know it. You are everything to me. You challenge me. You make me want to be a better man. If you'll have me, I promise to spend the rest of my life doing my best to deserve you. Will you marry me?"

"Yes. I will."

Chuck squeezed her hand. "I love you, sweetheart. Everything in my life changed when I met you and you spilled the iced tea on me at the diner."

She grinned and everyone chuckled.

"Immediately, I knew there was something special about you. Your sass, your laughter, your smile, and later I discovered how caring you are. Your heart is bigger than any I've ever known. Please make me the happiest man on the planet and marry me?"

"Yes. Yes. Yes." She kissed him and then kissed Lance. "I love you so very much."

The crowd cheered, and he knew that life had only just begun for him, Lance, and their new amazing bride-to-be.

The future had never looked brighter, a future in Wilde, Nevada, his new hometown.

THE END

WWW.CHLOELANG.COM

ABOUT THE AUTHOR

Born in Missouri, I am happy to call Dallas, Texas, home, now. Who doesn't love sunshine?

I began devouring romance novels during summers between college semesters as a respite to the rigors of my studies. Soon, my lifelong addiction was born, and to this day, I typically read three or four books every week.

For years, I tried my hand at writing romance stories, but shared them with no one. Understand, I'm really shy. After many months of prodding by friends, authors Sophie Oak and Kiera West, I finally relented and let them read one. As the prodding turned to gentle shoves, I ultimately did submit something to Siren-BookStrand. The thrill of a life happened for me when I got the word that my book would be published.

I do want to warn the reader that my books are not for the faint of heart, and are strictly for adults. That said, I love erotic romances. Blending the sexual chemistry with the emotional energy between the characters in my books is why I love being a writer.

For all titles by Chloe Lang, please visit
www.bookstrand.com/chloe-lang

Siren Publishing, Inc.
www.SirenPublishing.com

CPSIA information can be obtained at www.ICGtesting.com
Printed in the USA
LVOW04s1956300315

432595LV00023B/697/P